Gasping, she whirled to find Noah behind her, looking like some sort of fantasy come to life with his unbuttoned jeans, stubble-shadowed jaw and intense eyes.

The ebbing tide of adrenaline left her shaky, and her head sank onto his chest, caught the sharp intake of his breath. He ran a hand over her hair, keeping her safe in the solid circle of his arms. She drank in the pulse of his warmth, and her strung-up muscles started to unwind.

"Who was on the phone?" he asked, voice low and soothing.

She shook her head against his heated skin, wanted to fold herself right into him. "I don't know. But he doesn't like you. He ordered me to make you go away."

"He's picking on the wrong guy. I promise."

SYLVIE KURTZ

HONOR OF A HUNTER

HARLEQUIN®

TORONTO • NEW YORK • LONDON
AMSTERDAM • PARIS • SYDNEY • HAMBURG
STOCKHOLM • ATHENS • TOKYO • MILAN • MADRID
PRAGUE • WARSAW • BUDAPEST • AUCKLAND

For Chuck. Trustworthy, loyal, helpful,
friendly, courteous, kind, cheerful, brave.
You are all that and so much more.

A special thanks to: Joyce—for keeping me on pace.
Don and Patrick at Crimescene—for the crash course
on computer forensics. Ann—for being a terrific hostess
and showing me the sights of Seattle.

ISBN-13: 978-0-373-88802-3
ISBN-10:   0-373-88802-3

HONOR OF A HUNTER

Copyright © 2007 by Sylvie Kurtz

www.eHarlequin.com

Printed in U.S.A.

ABOUT THE AUTHOR

Flying an eight-hour solo cross-country in a Piper Arrow with only the airplane's crackling radio and a large bag of M&M's for company, Sylvie Kurtz realized a pilot's life wasn't for her. The stories zooming in and out of her mind proved more entertaining than the flight itself. Not a quitter, she finished her pilot's course and earned her commercial license and instrument rating.

Since then, she has traded in her wings for a keyboard, and she lets her imagination soar to create fictional adventures that explore the power of love and the thrill of suspense. When not writing, she enjoys the outdoors with her husband and two children, quilt-making, photography and reading whatever catches her interest.

You can write to Sylvie at P.O. Box 702, Milford, NH 03055. And visit her Web site at www.sylviekurtz.com.

Books by Sylvie Kurtz

HARLEQUIN INTRIGUE

*The Seekers

CAST OF CHARACTERS

Noah Kingsley—Seekers, Inc.'s computer expert is willing and able to use his skills to track down his best friend's stalker.

Faith Byrne—She wants to prove she's good enough to run the family business, but a stalker is stirring up more problems than she can handle on her own.

Philip Byrne—Faith's father is in the hospital recovering from a heart attack.

Griffin Egan—Faith's overprotective stepbrother isn't happy Faith brought in an expert to help her—not even if he's a friend with good intentions.

Tara Widrick—Griffin's paper-doll fiancée is jealous of the attention he gives his stepsister.

Sergio Sandoz—Faith's assistant understands her needs better than she does.

Max Hessel—Faith's neighbor has a new woman on his arm every week.

Kit Gadwah—The IT manager isn't happy Faith hired outside help to mess with his systems.

John Jaworski—Computers make him feel like a robot, and he's no fan of Faith's new inventory control program.

Neil Hardeman—Her father's right-hand man is ready for a different kind of game.

Bob Newsome—The married menswear manager has a wandering eye.

Chapter One

This was his favorite time of the day, that pause between the bustle of the workday and the final desertion into sleep. Night, with its thousands of lights, sparkled like it did on all the travel postcards he'd collected over the years.

A comfortable quiet suffused the apartment, and he roamed every room, taking in the details of her—the old-fashioned ticking of a grandfather clock in the entrance, the bouquet of irises on the living room coffee table, her penchant for pillows and throws and soft-to-the-touch fabrics. He trailed a finger here, a hand there, caressing the things that were hers, appreciating her sense of tradition and home.

In her bedroom, he bent to scoop up a discarded blouse. Details were her business.

Would she miss the blouse if he took it? He brought the silky dove-gray material she'd worn yesterday to his face and breathed in her scent. Roses and fresh linen. And ambition. He would have to tame that trait once they were married.

He folded the blouse and placed it on the chair of her vanity table. He'd have to teach her about proper housekeeping, too.

He glanced at the clock at her bedside. Past ten. She would be home any minute now. But that possibility only flooded his veins with the sweet adrenaline of anticipation.

He would reveal himself. Soon. But he wanted her to know the depth of his love first. When he pulled away the veil of mystery, she would say, *Of course. It had to be you.* Then she would smile and walk into his arms and they would tumble onto the satin sheets of her bed.

They were soul mates, meant to be together forever.

He closed his eyes and groaned, plunging his hands between her sheets, and imagined her nude form sliding against the blue satin, against him. From the moment he'd seen her, he'd thought of little else.

She would be his. They were fated to be together.

He pulled his hands away from the comfort of the cool satin and the intoxicating scent of her feminine perfume, and carefully extracted the three miniature hothouse orchids from the pocket of his jacket. Tiny blooms of pink perfections, just like her.

He ambled back to the living room. One last little present to let her know he was thinking of her. Soon she would have no choice. She would have to turn to him. And he would be there, arms wide open, to receive her.

The whir of the private elevator registered. Her? His heart did a quick dance. What if he stayed? What if he told her he loved her? No, she wasn't ready. Not yet.

He kissed the orchids and arranged them just so. She would love them. Then he added one last touch.

The key turned in the lock.

He smiled.

Welcome home, my love.

FAITH BYRNE PUSHED open the steel-core door to her condo and let out a sigh that drained away the bottled-up tension that had made her head pound and her shoulders scream and her feet ache. She didn't have two functioning brain cells left to put a cohesive thought together, let alone a long overdue dinner. Microwave popcorn would have to do. Again.

Nights like these, after an endless day, made the two million she'd spent on the twenty-second-floor penthouse seem like a bargain. Home. She was finally home.

She relocked the door behind her and entered her code on the alarm pad. Shedding her four-inch Manolo heels that added needed height to her five-foot-three frame, and the charcoal suit jacket with no-nonsense lines that were supposed to add authority to the squeaky-clean face even makeup couldn't make look grown-up, she crossed the Brazilian cherry floor to those awe-inspiring views of Elliott Bay that had made her fall in love with the place.

She flopped onto the club chair that wrapped around her in raspberry-colored marshmallow softness, and lost herself in the wide black swatch of the sky outside her floor-to-ceiling windows. The slow winking of stars and the festive twinkling of lights from the ships slowly drifting along the bay made her forget the crazy, busy madness of the day and believe that everything would turn out right.

Pulling a fleecy throw around her shoulders, she sighed again. Her detour to the hospital on the way home wasn't encouraging. Her father seemed to be slipping instead of improving, and the doctors couldn't pinpoint why. The disappointing October sales report wasn't going to do anything to speed his recovery either.

With only one store, Byrne's would never roar through the retail world with Godzilla power, but her efforts were paying off; Byrne's was finally starting to maximize its brand locally with its distinctive line of products. She was working on accomplishing the same success with their online presence, only to have some of her father's recent decisions plunge them back into the red.

She didn't want to be swallowed up by a stronger competitor, or worse, see her family's heritage die like so many other historic family-owned retailers. The tactics that were successful two generations ago when her grandfather had started the store weren't going to work in today's fast-forward world. If only she could make her father understand that without him shutting her out.

As crass as it sounded, while he was out of commission, she had her chance to prove she could manage the store efficiently—put it back in solid black—and make him proud. Maybe then, he'd see he could retire—or at least slow down—without a worry, that the store's future and the family's honor were in good hands.

Reflex had her reaching for the remote on the coffee table to catch the eleven o'clock headlines before crawling into bed. Six would come around faster than she wanted. If she was going to keep her promise to pull off a minor miracle, she'd need sleep. She aimed the remote at the plasma TV in the corner, but her thumb never pressed the power button.

Three pink orchids hung their perfect tiny heads from the television's rim, the blush of their plump lips both exquisite and obscene. Below them, etched in the dust of the screen were the words, "I'm watching you."

Someone had been here.

She jumped to her feet and spun around. The throw whirled off her shoulders and landed at her feet like a molted skin. Was he still here? The urgent whispers of menace swarmed over her scalp and down her spine, chilling her blood. Her gaze flittered over the open floor plan of her condo.

No movement in the nook. None in the kitchen. Only the slow ticking of her grand-mother's clock in the entrance, beating an ominous pulse. Nobody was here. Nothing to fear.

Then why was her mind manufacturing the musky odor of male sweat in the air?

The alarm hadn't been tripped. All the doors were still locked tight. There had to be a logical explanation.

Someone probably scrawled those words in the dust as a joke. But then where had the orchids come from? They hadn't been there this morning—or at least she didn't think they had. She'd overslept and left in a mad rush. Who would have done such a thing anyway? It wasn't as if she had company over every night. This was her haven. She couldn't remember the last time she'd invited anyone up.

Her father's voice boomed in her head. *Don't make a fuss. Don't make a scene.*

Was she just being paranoid? Maybe, but it didn't hurt to check.

Armed with the remote, she strode to the phone beside her stash of take-out menus and called the security desk in the lobby. "Hi, Albert, this is Faith Byrne in 2201. Was anyone up to my condo today?"

Computer keys clacked with brisk efficiency as Albert searched for the information she'd requested. "No, Ms. Byrne. No visitors. No deliveries. The housekeeping service won't be in until tomorrow and the gardener until Friday. Is there a problem?"

Don't make a fuss. Don't make a scene. We take care of our own problems privately. We don't splash them all over the headlines.

"No, thank you, Albert." But the clutch knotting her chest wouldn't let go. Someone had been in her home. Someone had broken through the fortress of a lobby manned by a security guard, an elevator that required a special security key card, her locked and bolted door, and an alarm system.

Call the police, Faith. What if he's still here?

If he was still here, she argued with herself, *he'd have shown himself.*

Or he could be waiting. The much too

vivid image of a shadowed stranger hiding in the closet, watching, waiting, sped a rush of ice down her body.

What if he's outside on the terrace right now?

She spun around to the living room. The white sheers that gave the room a light and airy feel now seemed too transparent. He could be there, hiding behind one of the huge terra-cotta pots that dotted the terrace. That both the door lock and safety lock on the slider track were engaged didn't reassure her. The open expanse of the condo made her feel like exposed prey.

Don't make a fuss. Don't make a scene.

I'm watching you.

Someone's been here.

She scrunched her eyes against her father's imagined displeasure. "On second thought, Albert, please call the police. I believe someone's broken into my condo."

"Right away, Ms. Byrne. Do you want Eddie to come up and wait with you?"

Eddie, the building's second security guard, on duty in the garage. "That would be great, thank you."

This couldn't be happening. Not to her.

Armed with a butcher knife, huddled and shaking in the nook with a clear view of her whole living space, including the terrace doors, she waited.

WHEN THE PHONE RANG, Noah Kingsley grabbed for it instinctively and mumbled, "What?" into the receiver. If someone was stupid enough to wake him in the dead of night, they didn't deserve politeness.

"Noah? It's Faith."

Noah shot up, heart pounding, wide awake. He snapped on the light on his bedside table and shoved on his glasses. "What's wrong?"

"Does anything have to be wrong?" Her attempt at lightness fell flat. Something *was* wrong.

He squinted at the alarm clock. "It's three-eleven in the morning and the last time you called this late…"

He let the rest of the sentence fall away, sure Faith wouldn't want a reminder of her state of hysteria the night two years ago when she'd caught Heath Jamieson, her father-approved husband of less than forty-eight hours, cheating on her with one of the cruise ship's chorus girls.

"I'm sorry," Faith said. "I didn't realize what time it was."

Forcing his heart to slow down, Noah leaned against the headboard. "Talk to me, Faith."

She let out a long breath. "I'm probably making something out of nothing."

"Molehills are your specialty," he teased, working hard to infuse his voice with the friend quality she expected when all he wanted to do was crawl into bed next to her and hold her tight. "What happened?"

She let out a roll of nervous laughter, dismissing her fears. He could imagine her raking her long fingers through her blond hair, squinting her pale topaz-blue eyes, the way she tended to do when she was confused. "Someone broke into my condo. Or I should say, materialized in and out of my home, since there were no signs of forced entry."

"What made you suspicious?" He knew she'd called because she wanted to counterbalance her stormy sea of emotions with his dependable logic, but man, oh, man, keeping free and easy was going to scrape another layer off his already raw heart. E-mails were easier, safer. *And who do you have to blame for that?* No one. Ever since the day her father had dragged her away from camp, he'd tried, he'd really tried, to pretend that being friends was good enough for him.

"The orchids left on the TV and the 'I'm watching you' fingered into the dust."

A punch of foreboding tightened Noah's gut, making him sit up straight. He was used to playing the sounding board to her emotional emergencies—all those times she'd failed to impress her father, all the bumps on the road of her rocky love life. He should cut off communications cold turkey, stop this torture, but he couldn't seem to help himself. He'd rather have this part of Faith than none at all. But this sounded different. Could she be in real trouble this time? "Has something like this happened before?"

"No, this was the first time." A hiccup of hesitation. "At home."

He didn't like the sound of that. "What happened at work?"

"I've been getting all sorts of weird e-mail messages. It's like this guy thinks he knows me and that we're having a conversation."

"Do you answer him?"

"No, I thought he was just a kook, and I didn't have time to deal with his crazy ideas, so I dismissed him."

"What kind of crazy ideas?" Obsession with Faith was something Noah understood only too well.

"Like changing our market slice to compete directly with Nordstrom. He doesn't seem to understand that if we stick with our Pioneer Square roots, even if we aren't technically there anymore, we have a better chance of survival."

"Sounds like someone who knows you. Someone you work with."

"From the store?" Her voice tore like canvas.

"He has to be close enough to you to know the workings of the store. Are the messages coming internally?"

"Not from Byrnes.com. They're from someone who calls himself FaithFan with a Yahoo! address."

Definitely not good. "Did you call the police?"

"About the e-mails? No. As for tonight…" She snorted. "For all the good that did. According to the officer, there was no implied threat. There were no signs of forced entry.

Nothing was stolen—except for my sense of safety, but that, apparently, doesn't count. And then there's the fact that I don't know who left the message. The officer's advice boiled down to, 'Call us when somebody does something.'"

Which, he'd learned over his years working with the system, was unfortunately too common of a response. He hated the thought of Faith alone and scared. "I'm not exactly next door, Faith. Isn't there anyone in Seattle you could call?"

"Not really." Faith uttered a choked sound. "How did I get like this? How did I end up so alone?"

"Work." Trying to please Daddy, not realizing that Daddy would never be pleased. She should have struck out on her own years ago. He plucked the extra pillow across his stomach and held on to it tight. Not his place to tell the old man where to go. Faith had to break the chains herself, or the pressure of her father's misguided will would always yank her back.

"Pathetic, huh?"

"Ambitious. Determined. Driven." He wished he could snap his fingers and make everything right for her, make her trust her own bright light, make her see that she was too good to keep begging for her father's approval.

"You always did know the right thing to say."

Except twelve years ago, when he'd believed all the accusations spewed his way, when he'd believed he deserved to lose her, when heaven had turned into hell, and he wasn't sure how it all had happened.

"You're the only person I can trust, Noah. Everybody else in my life wants something from me."

Like her father who'd wanted a son. Like Heath who'd married her for her money. Noah wasn't immune either.

"What about Camp Cat Fight?" he asked. "I wanted something then."

She gave a small laugh at their nickname for Camp Ketchum-Fitch. "Um, if I recall, *you* were the one reluctant to get out of his khaki shorts, and *I* had to charm them off of you."

Reluctant wasn't the word he'd use. He'd fallen hard for Faith the second his gaze had landed on her across the bonfire at the mixer between Camp Ketchum-Fitch and Camp Ninnuok where he'd worked as a Boy Scout counselor. In the open windows to her soul, he'd seen the promise of mystery and laughter and excitement, and that potent combination had drawn him in helplessly. He'd wanted her so fiercely all that summer that it had petrified him. "Let's just say the charming was mutual."

"I'm scared, Noah."

And he knew admitting as much was taking a chunk out of her pride. "Tell you what. You lock your doors, batten down the windows, then go to bed, and I'll stay on the line with you."

"You'd do that?"

I'd do anything for you. Don't you know that by now? "While we talk, I'll see if the jet is available."

"You don't have to fly all the way out here."

He reached for the laptop that had somehow migrated to the foot of his bed after he'd fallen asleep. "Come on, shortcake." Did she still taste like sweet strawberries and cream? *Don't go there, Noah. You're the friend, remember?* He shook his head and booted up the laptop. "You have access to one of the best computer wizards in the country. Why not make use of his expertise to track down your stalker?"

"I'm probably making too much of this." But the clicks and clacks told him she was checking locks and windows anyway. "Do you really think I'm being stalked?"

"You're getting unwanted, repeated messages from someone you don't know. He's somehow invaded your home security and made you feel unsafe. That's called stalking, and it's something you have to stop right now before it escalates."

"Do you think I'm in danger?"

"He broke into your home, Faith. He left a threat on your television dust."

The sound of her hard swallow carried across the country. "I'll call the police again in the morning."

Noah pulled up the Kingsley Enterprises page and logged on. "Before you do, here's what you need to do. Take a photo of the message on your television dust."

"I haven't replaced my camera yet."

The one she'd thrown at Heath when she'd found him cheating. "On your cell phone?"

"Okay."

"Make a copy of all the electronic data

he's sent you and copy it onto two CDs—one for the police and one for me. Keep the CDs in a safe place. He's shown he can get into your condo, and he could erase the traces of his harassment if he thinks he's being cornered."

"And I'd have no proof—as little as it is."

"Right." Noah clicked on the corporate jet icon and checked the schedule. "If he gets in touch with you before I get there, I want you to answer him once, and only once, with a message that says, 'Leave me alone. Stop harassing me. Do not contact me again.' That establishes that contact is unconsented. Don't, for any reason, ever reply to anything else he sends." Amazing all he'd learned about stalking while poring over Brynna Reed's computers last June when her brother got himself—and her—in a pickle.

"Got it."

"And start putting together a log of dates, times, locations, circumstances of each incident of contact."

He could probably give Faith the name of a dozen people as equally qualified as he was in Seattle—his friend, Ben Lovan, for one. But he wouldn't. Faith was in danger. He'd get on his white jet and fly to her rescue, because she could still make him want to give her the moon even if he could never have her.

"I want you to feel safe," he said, sounding like a concerned friend, feeling anything but. He wanted the right to rage at her attacker, the right to force her into protective custody, and, damn it, the right to love her. "I can trace whoever's bothering you through his cyber footprints." And make him wish he'd never started bothering Faith. "Once we know who it is, then we can stop him." Crush him like a cockroach so he never does this to anyone again. "I'm up for a vacation, and I haven't been to Seattle in ages. I'm thinking you could treat me to a salmon dinner, and we'll call it even."

"You have to let me pay your expenses."

He frowned at the unexpected firecracker that burst in him. How could she want to *pay* him? "We're friends, Faith."

"Yes, we are. And you're right. I trust you. It's an efficient solution to a touchy problem. Especially with all that's going on right now."

Yeah, that was him all right. An efficient

solution to a problem. Everybody's friend, everybody's brother. "What else is going on?"

The sound of her footfalls shifted from wood to carpet. "I told you about Dad's heart attack, didn't I?"

She hadn't. "When did that happen?"

"Last week. He just keeled over right in the middle of the department-head meeting. We got him to the hospital in time, but he's still not responding the way the doctors expected."

Even dead, Noah doubted Philip Byrne could quite cut the steel strings of control he had over Faith. "Your dad's a tough bird. He'll pull through."

"I know."

The slide of skin on sheets slinked much too enticingly through the line, reviving images of Faith and moonlight and the best and worst day of his life. Was her room as girly as she was in her heart of hearts? Or had she gone for the cold, efficient look her father preferred simply to please him? *Not a good place to go, Noah.* Faith saw him as just a friend, and if he wanted some part of her in his life, he'd have to accept her terms.

"I've put in for the jet," he said as he confirmed the availability. Next he checked on weather and computed a flight plan. "Can you meet me at Boeing Field? I'll need a ride."

"Just let me know what time."

He switched to his electronic calendar. "I have a meeting early in the morning, but I'll call you as soon as it's over and let you know my ETA. And don't tell anyone about me."

"Why not?"

Because if her stalker saw him as competition, it could escalate the danger for Faith. "I need to do some research. I don't want to inflame the situation. I may need to come up with a cover that won't spook him."

"Oh."

"I'll need a list of your employees."

"All one hundred and eighty of them?"

"Until we can start narrowing down the field everybody is under suspicion."

His fingers played the keyboard, hoping that he was wrong, that he was making too much of Faith's problem because it involved her and, when it came to Faith, his judgment wasn't exactly based on logic. "So other than the stalking and the heart attack, how's everything going?"

"Isn't that enough?"

More than, but Faith didn't know when to

say no, especially when it came to Byrne's. "What's it like being the big boss?"

He could feel her sagging into soft pillows, and remembered the warm weight of her body curled against his, so perfect, so right, and he silently cursed her father.

Her sigh vibrated in his ear, tripped another wire of need he didn't want. "I'm finding out the hard way that being taken seriously in the world of big-boy business when you look like Barbie's little sister isn't easy. But I've been making headway in the past week. Dad's dogs are learning that I'm now where the buck stops. No going over my head to Philip Byrne to get the final okay."

"That's my girl. I never had a doubt you could do it."

"I'm not there yet." She yawned. "With the holiday shopping season coming fast, I've been working overtime. The day-after-Thanksgiving sale *has* to go off without a hitch."

Overtired and overstressed. But Noah had learned that traps mined the field of his friendship with Faith. And the subject of "Daddy" was the number one misstep that could blow the whole fragile sod to nothing. "Go to sleep."

"I can't." But already her voice was taking on a drowsy edge. "Tell me what's been going on with you. How are your sisters?"

"Meredith's still trying to be the perfect wife, mother and Realtor. Joanna's still spending all of her time at the hotel or at horse shows."

"They both love what they're doing."

There was a lesson for Faith there, but he wasn't about to mention that either. "They do."

"Are Reed and Abbie back from their honeymoon?"

"Reed's been wearing a goofy grin ever since. If you ask me, it won't be long before they start a family." Noah rolled his shoulders at the sudden weight crunching them.

In a breezy tone, he caught Faith up on all the news with his fellow Seekers—about Mercer's adventure in the White Mountains with Nora, Skyralov's misadventures at playing dad while Luci was attending the police academy, and about the continuing courtship between Falconer and Liv, who couldn't remember her original romance with her husband because of a brain injury, and was determined to have a past before she renewed her vows.

And all the while Noah kept shifting uneasily on the bed that had suddenly become uncomfortable.

Twelve years ago, his mind full of adventure, he hadn't been looking for love. Then *wham*—there she was. *The* one. The one he was going to spend the rest of his life with. For that one fleeting summer, they'd both thought so.

How wrong they'd both been.

He kept talking long after she'd fallen asleep, until the light of dawn crept through the slats of his shades and slashed the stripes on his navy comforter with shadows, until the alarm strobed on, shaking him out of his folly. A folly that even the cold, hard light of day couldn't quite dissipate.

"Faith?" he said into the silence on the other end of the line. "I have to go now. I've set up a ring tone just for you on my cell phone." As he spoke he sent a text message to her cell phone and an e-mail to both her work and personal addresses with his number. "If you need anything, just call. Anytime. I'll see you this afternoon."

AT THE AERIE, Seekers, Inc.'s headquarters, Noah cornered Falconer after the morning briefing in the basement bunker. The scent of strong coffee and Liv's apple-oatmeal muffins lingered in the air, giving the room the feel of home rather than work. "Can you do without me for a week?"

Falconer cocked a dark eyebrow at him. "I can. But do I want to?"

Noah ignored the fact Falconer saw right through the verbal games that usually caught most people off guard and got Noah his way. "Harper should be able to handle the computers without causing too much damage." Reed was useless with technology, Mercer's broken hand was still on the mend, and Skyralov worked shortened hours these days. "If he gets in over his head, he can always call my cell. I'll leave it on."

"What's up?"

Noah shrugged indifferently, trying not to squirm under Falconer's too-keen gaze. Noah never made demands. He was always on call and on time, going above and beyond—except for the weekend or two he'd taken off over the summer to bag a few four-thousand-footers. Falconer had no complaints about his performance. He had no reason to deny Noah's reasonable request.

"An old friend needs my computer expertise." The less said on the topic of Faith, the better.

Smile. Let Falconer think none of this was any big deal.

As always, Falconer saw right through the smoke and mirror of words, but he let the illusion live, knowing that content workers returned the favor with loyalty. "Get Harper up to speed before you leave."

"Will do."

"Stay in touch."

"Roger."

Noah rounded up his laptop, cell phone and PDA, and raided Seekers' cache of electronic gadgets, almost wishing Falconer had given him an out. Better all around if someone else helped Faith.

But she was being stalked. She was in danger. He couldn't trust anyone else with her life.

What did that make him? *A masochist, that's what.*

Noah paused as he dumped his equipment next to the duffel bag already waiting in the trunk of his Outback. *This is crazy. Why are you doing this to yourself?*

Because Faith needs help.

And maybe, just maybe, if he went to her, he could get her out from under his skin and finally move on. She belonged to Byrne's, and he belonged here with the mountains and his music and his computers.

He slammed shut the hatchback. If he was going to pull off the good-friend-only act, he'd need to strap on a bulletproof vest over his heart.

Because Faith was the one thing in his life he couldn't battle with logic.

Chapter Two

Faith paced the length of the tall windows looking out over the crisscross of runways and taxiways at the King County International Airport, still known as Boeing Field. The blue sky was clear enough to show off Mount Rainier, but she wasn't in the mood to admire its majesty. Each time a corporate jet landed, her heart thumped in anticipation. Each time Noah failed to exit the jet, her heart sank to her toes.

Then there he was, and suddenly she wasn't ready. What if he was disappointed? What if she didn't measure up? What if—? *Stop it. Noah's not like that.*

People change, she argued.

Not Noah.

Dressed in khaki pants, a bottle-green shirt and a brown leather bomber-style jacket, he crossed the tarmac with an easy confidence he'd carried even as a sixteen-year-old. He held a duffel bag in one hand and had a messenger bag slung across his chest. At the terminal entrance, he took off his aviator-style glasses, rested them on top of his short, light brown hair, and looked around for her. His gaze connected with hers. Her breath caught in her chest, freezing her to the spot.

This wasn't going to work.

Her father, her grandmother, everyone who'd interfered with her private business with their unwanted advice had said teenage love didn't last. That she'd outgrow it. To please her father, she'd tried to be practical and adult and move on. In the end, he'd been right. Hers and Noah's goals had taken sharply different paths. But no other man could quite live up to that first blush of hormone-swamped passion she'd shared with Noah.

She'd written him piles of letters over the years, but mailed only pithy holiday greetings and birthday jokes and random e-mails that were general enough to apply to anyone. Their renewed phone calls over the past three years never addressed that once fervent passion. Friendship. They'd agreed on friendship. And in a world where she couldn't trust a soul, that one friendship meant everything.

Get over yourself, Faith. You're not sixteen. Noah is an expert, and you're simply consulting that expertise. That was what any businesswoman worth her six-figure salary would do.

He looked at her for a second as if soaking her in, and her heart beat in an almost forgotten bolero. Then a big, warm smile flooded his face and overflowed into his hazel eyes. A rush of heat rolled over her, making her wonder what she'd feared about seeing him again after so many years. He was her friend, and he'd come to help her. Simple as that.

She gave him a quick hug, fighting the urge to stay in the solid circle of his arms. The crook of her neck still fit perfectly in the curve of his shoulder, she noted, and his crisp mountain-air scent could still calm her ragged nerves. That wasn't chemistry sizzling between them, just relief that she wouldn't have to handle her stalker alone. "For a guy who's been flying all day, you look good."

"For a girl who didn't sleep much last night, you look positively radiant," he teased back.

"It's seeing you again." Her flippant tone denied the truth. She hooked an arm through his, melted into his lean-muscled body for just a second of comfort, then led him through the creamed-coffee lobby of the terminal. Her four-inch heels ringing against the tiles, she pushed through the glass doors and headed toward the parking lot. With him at her side, she felt as if she could take on the world and win. "I'll take you home. I have everything you asked for ready and—"

The rest of the sentence disappeared into the jet fuel–laced sea breeze as something shiny on the red hood of her car caught a glint of afternoon sun. The confidence that had boosted her only seconds ago shattered and left her shaking.

Three bullets sat on their flat ends, right down the middle of the hood, trembling under the deep-throated thrum of a departing jet's engines.

The message couldn't be clearer. Her stalker's obsession—which had taken on Everest-size magnitude in her mind since she'd discovered his existence last night—had crossed the line into violence. He wanted to kill her. Because of Noah? No, her stalker couldn't know she'd asked for help. No one did.

"I didn't tell anyone where I was going." Her arm gripped Noah's elbow in a vise. "Not even Sergio, my personal assistant. How could this creep know where I am?"

"Let's have a look."

Noah dropped the duffel, extricated himself from her grip and inspected the car, running his hands over every surface. He took off the messenger bag, handed her his leather jacket and slid under the undercarriage, not caring that his khaki pants were getting smeared with dirt. He shoved back out and asked her to pop the hood. Swearing, he fought with something near the radiator. A minute later, a triumphant look beaming over his face, he held up a small black box. "Looks like somebody does love you, shortcake."

"A tracking device?"

Noah nodded, turning the box over in his hands as if it were a puzzle he had to figure out. "Looks like some sort of GPS. Probably monitors the car's movements through a computer. Maybe even a cell phone." He shook his head. "Technology's taken stalking to brand-new heights."

Her icy arms tightened around Noah's jacket, squeezing a reassuring cloud of his outdoors-fresh scent. She closed her eyes and shook her head. "This is a nightmare."

"Take heart. He's already given up more about himself than he thinks. He's technology savvy, and has a bank account big enough to afford the latest toys."

She gulped and fixed her gaze on the neat row of bullets. "And he has access to guns."

Noah's face sobered. He scooped the bullets into a handkerchief he drew out of his jacket pocket and stuffed them into his messenger bag and out of her line of vision. "Any idea who would want to keep such close tabs on you?"

"None." In spite of her desire to appear firmly in control, panic leaked into her voice. She couldn't help it; she surveyed the parking lot. "Do you think the creep is here? Watching us?" Was her fear feeding his deluded fantasy?

"Let's find out."

Faith raised one eyebrow. "What do you have in mind?"

"Let's go for a ride."

She looked at her beloved Porsche as if it had suddenly grown flesh-ripping talons. The pull-me-over-red Boxter had seemed like such a good idea after Heath's betrayal when she'd needed the feel of speed and power and had wanted to scream at the top of her lungs, "Hey, look at me, I'm here!" Now it was a neon light in a sea of black and silver sedans. How could anyone have missed it? She was making it too easy for her stalker to find her.

"Stop beating yourself over the head," Noah said, as if reading her mind. "You didn't do anything wrong."

He took his jacket and the keys from her, settled her into the passenger's seat and slipped into the driver's seat. He slanted her a mischievous grin and waggled an eyebrow. "Tell me where to go."

She gave a small laugh and shook her head. Where she wanted him to go was impossible. Their lives had grown too far apart. He couldn't leave his world any more than she could hers. And they'd made a pact. She couldn't risk losing his friendship over a weakness of character. "You could always make me laugh, even when there was nothing to laugh at." She jerked her chin toward the exit. "Get on the freeway going north."

He did as she directed, piloting the Boxter

expertly in the hairy Seattle traffic with his steady nerve, quick hands and smooth pedal work. Watching him practically purr at the car's performance, she was glad she'd opted for the manual transmission. As she watched his confident profile, some of the wire-tight tendons at the back of her neck let go a little. "Thanks for coming to my rescue."

"We'll find him."

Placing her hands flat between her knees, she nodded. If anyone could perform that miracle, it was Noah. "Is anyone following us?"

"Not yet."

He pulled off I-5 and into a gas station parking lot, then handed her some change. "Why don't you get me a Dr Pepper?"

"I thought you didn't drink soda."

"Only when I'm training."

"Cross-country skiing, right?"

"Dr Pepper." Noah tossed his head toward the squat building that served as a convenience store. "Original—not that diet stuff you like."

She hesitated, then sighed. "Okay, I'll be right back."

By the time she came back out, he was leaning against the front quarter panel of her car waiting for her, a satisfied expression on his face. She handed him his soda. "So who's the lucky winner?"

"I thought of sending it to Canada with a retired couple." He twisted his gaze toward a Winnebago two pumps down sporting a bumper sticker that read, *We're spending our kids' inheritance.* "But then I thought that if the guy wasn't stable—"

She snorted. "Obviously he's not."

"I didn't want them hurt."

Typical Noah, and it made her heart both fly and sink. The image of the bullets on the hood of her car flashed into her mind. What if she'd led *him* into danger? "So?"

"So, it's on its way south on a truck with mud wheels and an ATV in the bed. The driver's burly and mean-looking enough to take care of himself."

He popped open the can of soda and took a long pull. "Got hooked on this stuff when I was in El Paso."

Usually she faced problems head-on, but right now she wanted to pretend it didn't exist, that she wasn't being stalked, that Noah was here not to save her, but to— *Forget it, Faith. Don't ruin the one good thing you've got going.* "How long were you there? El Paso?"

"Too long."

She cocked her head in question.

"Too hot. No snow."

"You know most people dream of living in a place where it's warm all year around."

That boyish smile again—the one that had haunted her dreams too many nights. She was glad he hadn't outgrown it.

"There's your answer right there." He lobbed the empty soda can into the trash bin.

He was right. He wasn't like most people. He wasn't like anyone she knew. He didn't do the expected just because it was expected. He was strong enough to follow his heart, his dreams. Her bank account and future inheritance held no interest to him. Wasn't that why she could trust him?

"So what do we do next?" She rolled the water bottle between her hands. Try as she might, she couldn't forget those three bullets. What had they meant? "It won't take him long to figure out I'm not on that southbound truck."

"It buys me some time to get up to speed." He straightened and opened the passenger door. "Talk to me, Faith."

Back on the highway, with the soothing roll of tires on asphalt and the pulse of rush hour traffic, she spilled the insanity tainting the ordered plan of her life.

"YOU KNOW, HOMELAND SECURITY strongly suggests you keep three days' worth of food and water in your home in case of an emergency," Noah said after the hostess had shown them to their table at the Emerald City Waterfront Grill and Brew Pub, which didn't look like any brew pub Noah had ever gone to. Plush chairs were ensconced in semiprivate cocoons, most with a view of Elliott Bay. The decor was hunter-green and white, except for the red carnations in the vases on the table. The sun was melting on the water, turning it into a brilliant ripple of orange-red.

"If disaster struck," Faith said, worrying the corner of the leather-covered menu, "I'd most likely be at the store, and the café there has enough food to keep me alive and kicking for three days."

A basket of crusty rolls and a plate of garlic-and-basil dipping oil appeared, and he pushed it toward her. Judging by the empty state of the pantry in her condo, she desperately needed a decent meal. Noah would give her time to settle and eat before broaching the subject of finding her stalker. She'd given him some details, but he'd have to dig deeper, and the thought of seeing the worry lines already pleating Faith's forehead deepen didn't appeal to him.

He wanted to see her smile, hear her laugh—the way she had that summer, bringing so much sunshine into his world. He should have known a light so bright would burn. But he knew the boundaries this time, and he was prepared. "Whatever happened to your Greek shipping heir, Niklos Whatshisname?"

"We broke up." She shook her head and tore a roll in two. "Can you believe there are people who never work?"

He exaggerated a gasp. "Shocking."

"You're making fun of me."

"Only a little bit."

He settled on the Copper River salmon and a local beer, and she on the sole and white wine. He ate, and she picked at the sole, flaking the filet into hash with the tines of her fork.

"You can't let the bastard get to you,"

Noah said. "That's what he wants. That's how he's going to control you."

Her pale blue eyes hardened to ice. "I can't get those bullets out of my mind. That's more than stalking. That's a threat."

"I'm not going to let anyone hurt you." He gestured at her plate. "You need to eat."

She shook her head. "I can't."

Letting out a long sigh, she resumed her destruction of the sole. "So how are we going to find…*him?*"

The stalker. The bullet-leaving piece of scum who was scaring her. So much for waiting until she had food in her. Suddenly the salmon didn't taste as good as it had a bite ago, and he put down his fork. "I'll need to look at your computer at work and at home and see what that gives us."

"Do you think he left a trace behind?"

"They always do. Depending on how smart he is, though, he could try to hide his tracks."

"But you can still find him?"

"I'll give it my best shot."

"What if…" She twirled her wineglass in small circles on the white tablecloth, looking into the pale gold liquid as if willing it to give her answers. "What if he's hidden too well?"

"Then we'll hunt him the old-fashioned way. He's leaving physical evidence now. The GPS unit has a serial number. The orchids don't look like the garden-variety kind. The note in the dust." The damn bullets for a 9 mm pistol. "It's someone here in Seattle. Someone who knows you."

"That doesn't make me feel any better."

"But it narrows the net of possibilities."

She drew in a breath, shaking her head. "I can't imagine anyone I know who'd do something like this."

He could. With her gentle girl-next-door features, her wide blue eyes and the sweet sweep of freckles dusting her nose, she looked like a soft mark. Odds were her stalker had already approached her, and she'd most likely rebuffed him, unaware he was making advances. Faith's focus on goals was single-minded, especially when it came to Byrne's. "Your dad's dogs aren't happy about you taking over the day-to-day operations at Byrne's."

"It's a family business. That family takes over is normal, expected."

"That doesn't prevent jealousy or the feeling of entitlement by the old guard." He'd heard enough horror stories from his sisters after his father retired and handed them the reins to the businesses he'd grown into a small empire. And Roger Kingsley was a man loved by all, while Philip Byrne tended to rule by fear.

Faith shrugged one shoulder. "That's true, I suppose."

"Tell me about the people most likely to resent your new role."

She crushed the last of the sole and set her fork down. "Neil Hardeman's been my father's right-hand man for as long as I can remember. But he's always crashing his computers, so I doubt he's the one sending the messages.

"The receiving manager's been vocal about the new inventory control system we're trying to get up and running, but John doesn't have the agility to climb twenty-two flights of stairs and leave me presents in my apartment.

"The guy who runs the IT department would know how to use the computer, but Kit couldn't care less who he works for as long as he gets to run his department his way."

"I'll check them out."

As if she hadn't heard him, she frowned

down at the modern art she'd made out of her sole. "The fashion manager isn't too pleased at the direction I'm taking, but would she send flowers and write something like 'I'm watching you'?"

"Doesn't sound like a woman's kind of threat." Though these days women's prisons were as overcrowded as the men's. He hated seeing Faith so wound up. Where was the free-spirited girl who had dared him to defy camp rules and run away with her?

"I've gone out of my way not to be a bitch boss." Her head moved from side to side in a slow, continuous movement. "I'm nice to everyone. I don't whine and complain. I have an open-door policy. Anyone can come to me with a problem. I've implemented ideas brought to me *and* given the originator credit. I go out of my way to reward people and promote a team atmosphere. I can't imagine any of Byrne's employees hating me enough to want to kill me."

"You never know who holds a grudge or why." As he'd experienced with his job as a U.S. Marshal and with Seekers, Inc., love, hate, anger, hurt, greed—all those sticky human emotions—caused enough troubles to keep law enforcement busy in perpetuity. As much as his job dealt with facts, he'd learned to follow the trail of emotions, too. "Who has access to your condo?"

Her head continued its slow shake, as if each possibility added claws and fangs to her growing nightmare. "There's the gardener who maintains the terrace garden. I have a maid service that comes once every other week, but they don't have a key. The building manager lets them in."

A man entered the restaurant, his posture commanding the kind of attention an approaching lightning storm would. The perfectly coiffed dirty-blond hair, steel-colored eyes and tailored suit lent him a big-screen, leading-man quality. His six-foot frame loomed over the maître d's stand and his gaze had glommed onto Faith from the second he'd spotted her. Not unusual since she was a looker, but something about the icy stare raised Noah's hackles. "Give me a list of names. I'll run background checks on them. What about boyfriends?"

"None in the picture." The flat line of her mouth said that situation wasn't likely to change anytime soon.

"Has anyone shown any interest? Asked you out for a date? That type of thing."

"Not since the spring charity ball when my neighbor wanted to share a limo."

"Add him to the list."

The man strode purposefully toward Faith, tugging a paper-thin woman behind him and ignoring the path the hostess was taking toward the other end of the dining room. Noah pushed his chair back a hair, wishing his SIG wasn't back in New Hampshire. The man clamped a hand over Faith's shoulder and Noah stood, ready to pounce.

"Faith?"

Faith looked up and a smile exploded on her face. "Griffin! What are you doing here?"

Griffin pulled his paper-doll companion forward. "I'm taking Tara out to dinner."

Had poor Tara had a choice? On cue, Tara gave a plastic lift of over-plumped lips. Noah had wanted her eyes to be as vacant as her smile, but the blue shone with intelligence and seemed to run through a myriad calculations as fast as a supercomputer. She was no meek lamb to Griffin's blustery lion.

"I was surprised you weren't at the hospital when I stopped by," Griffin said.

A flutter of guilt wavered through Faith's eyes. "An old friend came into town unexpectedly. I'll visit Daddy later." She turned to Noah, the flick of her fingers against his ready hand seeming to say, *Stand down, he's no threat.* "Noah, this is my brother, Griffin Egan, and his fiancée, Tara Widrick." The amused glint in her eye said Tara was father-approved. "Griffin, Noah Kingsley."

Griffin scowled at Noah like a man used to being at the top of the food chain. Philip Byrne had trained his stepson well. "Why does that name sound familiar?"

"Kingsley Enterprises are big on the East Coast." Not that Noah had anything to do with his father's businesses. He'd never cared for corporate games or politics and had left that to his sisters who thrived on the pursuit. He liked the big outdoors and puzzles and high-tech gadgets—and outsmarting bad guys. That was something his father didn't get, but supported nonetheless. Still, when it came to impressing blowhards like Griffin, Noah wasn't above using his father's name to buy clout.

Griffin's eyebrows scrunched farther. "No, that's not it." Then he shook his head. "No matter. I'll figure it out. We'll let you finish your meal." He nodded dismissively at Noah. "Nice to meet you." He then held Faith in the magnetic grip of his gaze a shade too long. A warning? "See you in the morning, Faith."

Odds were Griffin planned to have words with Faith about her out-of-town friend. Great. The last thing Noah needed was to play tug-of-war with Faith's overprotective stepbrother. Which was why he generally preferred computers to people—less conflict.

Noah sat down, keeping Griffin and his paper-doll date in his peripheral vision. "I think you should take a leave from the store until your stalker's in jail. Griffin can handle things at Byrne's."

"Absolutely not." Faith banged a hand flat against the white tablecloth. "Griffin's good with money. Not so good with people."

No kidding. Noah felt sorry for his poor fiancée. "It's just for a few days. A week at most."

"This time of the year is too critical for the store." The pale pink shell of her nail emphasized each of her points. "After a solid back-to-school season, we saw a three point nine percent sales slide in October. If we don't do well between Thanksgiving and Christmas, we'll have to lay off people and cut back on programs that could make a huge difference in our market share. With Daddy sick, I can't drop the ball. He'd never forgive me."

And there was the rub. Daddy's approval.

Noah had figured out long ago that Faith was willing to give up just about anything for Byrne's. Which didn't leave him much choice. He'd have to stick by her side until the crisis was over.

That meant poring through her computer tonight while she slept and having a cover ready by morning. One that would allow him access to every employee, every computer and every minute of her day—and get past her stubborn pride by making it seem as if the whole thing was her idea.

No way Noah was letting Faith out of his sight while her stalker was still on the loose.

They left the restaurant, and Griffin's Velcro glare stuck to their track. Alongside the ebb and flow of downtown traffic, silence was their easy companion as they strolled the three blocks from the restaurant to Faith's condo. Brisk briny air teased Faith's hair, the way he wanted to, so he kept his hands fisted in his pockets and his gaze skipping over the architecture ranging from brick to glass all the way to her building.

The elevator doors opened on the twenty-second floor, and a man waited. He wasn't as ordered and precise as Griffin, but he had the same kind of flash. Upscale suit, gold watch, diamond ring, shiny shoes, slick black hair and an air that all but shouted, *Look at me*. His brilliant white teeth sparkled through his smile as he recognized one occupant. "Faith!"

"Hi, Max." To Noah she said, "Max Hessel, my neighbor. We share an elevator. Max, this is my friend, Noah Kingsley."

"Nice to meet you." Noah offered Max a hand and the other man's grip had too much starch. Was there history between Faith and Max? An affair that hadn't ended well, at least on his end? Faith had never mentioned a Max. But then Faith only called when she was hurt.

"About time you got yourself a 'friend.'" Max winked, then took their place in the elevator and pressed the lobby button. "Have yourself a really good night, babe."

"Don't mind Max." Faith handed Noah her key. "He's a jerk."

"A jerk with an interest in you?"

She laughed. "I'm definitely not his type."

"What's his type?"

"Easy."

Noah entered ahead of her and flipped on the lights while she took care of the alarm. "Maybe he's ready for a challenge."

"He's not into working that hard."

As the burst of light dazzled, movement in Noah's peripheral vision caught his attention. In the hallway mirror hung three folded-paper cranes on golden strings that hadn't been there before, waltzing under the furnace vent's hot breath. Their huge felt-pen eyes took up most of their heads, making their meaning clear.

I'm watching you.

Chapter Three

At the sight of the three cranes floating in the entrance mirror, Noah turned to Faith, ready to scoop her up and out of danger.

Her index finger was poised over the alarm pad, her eyes wide and her mouth cracked open in a silent gasp. The pink blush the November wind had painted on her cheeks leached out of her skin, leaving it an unhealthy white.

"H-he got in again," she stammered. "How?"

Her breath escaped in a long whoosh, and its stutter hit him right in the solar plexus. Heart wedged in his throat, Noah examined the lock. His indifference might seem cold, but she was counting on him to stay cool, to find a solution to her problem. That calm, cool solution was the one thing he could give to her. "No signs of forced entry. Get the alarm before it triggers."

Too late. The phone rang. Faith reached for the receiver on the table beneath the gilt-framed mirror. "I'm fine," she said in answer. "But could you call the police?"

Steering wide of Faith's wounded-deer eyes, Noah closed the front door and cleared the rest of the apartment while she spoke to the security guard, but he saw no other disturbance. The slider was still locked and bolted, as was the door that led to the emergency stairway.

"The police are on their way." Faith stared at the gliding cranes, her arms knotted tight under her chest, and a searing ache to soothe her twitched all the way down to his fingers.

"He can't just *materialize*," she said.

"Someone must have a key." Keeping his back to Faith, he examined the cranes with every ounce of attention he could muster. His bones could still feel her trembling, and he had to fight the powerful urge to speed her away from danger. Biting back a curse, he re-focused on his task. Plain copy paper. He'd bet the police lab would find no prints. "Can you get the camera out of my bag? I want to take pictures before the police arrive."

She nodded and went to a white desk with curvy legs in a nook between her living room and kitchen where he had left his bag. The desk was neat, but not stuffy. Strong, yet feminine. Just like she was.

"The only other person with a key is the building manager." She rummaged through his messenger bag. "And I change the security code every time I expect him to come up to let the maid service or the gardener in."

"Where do you keep your keys?" He took the digital camera she handed him, ignoring the icy feel of her flesh when their fingers touched.

"Usually in this bowl when I'm home." She pointed to the multicolored glass monstrosity sitting on the accent table under the mirror. "In my purse in my office when I'm at work."

And she had an open-door policy. "Someone could have gone into your office and made a copy while you were somewhere else in the building."

She shuddered, and the little hitch in her breath chinked another dent in the armor he thought he'd put around his heart.

He grabbed a pen from his pocket and made a note on the index card he always carried.

Keep on task. Facts. Evidence. Not Faith. "Three orchids. Three bullets. Three cranes. Have you received anything else in threes?"

She shook her head, and a new flash of fear launched her into motion.

"At work?"

Her ragged pacing of the cherrywood floor between the foyer and the living room betrayed the frustration needling at her. "I can't think—" She stopped and whirled to face him. "Wait. There was the basket of fruit I got in the middle of the back-to-school promotion. Three apples. Three pears. Three oranges."

"Was there a card with the basket?"

Frowning, she rubbed at her arms as if the overheated condo held no warmth. "Yes, but there was no name on it. I remember thinking it had come from one of our sales accounts, and it bothered me because I couldn't send a thank-you note."

And propriety was a big thing with Faith. He almost smiled. "Do you still have the card?"

She shook her head. "I didn't think it was important. I don't know how much help it would've been anyway. It was computer-printed. No logo or anything. Just 'Eat Healthy' in capital letters."

"Maybe it's not related."

Remembering something else, she flapped a finger at him. "There was a cake sent from the store's café on my birthday in October. It had three dark chocolate coins on top and three white candles."

"Does the café usually send you a cake on your birthday?"

A pucker formed between her eyebrows. "Come to think of it, they sent two. I thought it was because they'd gotten the first one wrong. You know, three candles, one for each decade—except that I turned twenty-eight, not thirty."

"The second one had twenty-eight candles."

She nodded, distracted. The way she looked around the apartment made him think that everything was starting to look suspicious—even the three loose paper clips on her desktop, which she brushed into her palm and threw away. "What's with three anyway?"

Damned if he knew. "Something that has meaning for him."

She was pacing again, chewing on a thumbnail. Her compact body thrummed with so much tension, it wound around him from across the room. He shut himself off by adjusting the camera's focus on the cranes and snapping picture after picture.

"How could I not have noticed the pattern?" she asked, her voice a thread about to break. "All these months of obliviousness."

"You had no reason to. You get gifts and samples all the time. It's part of the business."

"But—"

This time, he couldn't help it; he put the camera down, reached for her arms to stop her frantic motion and looked into the clear blue pools of her eyes. "No buts, Faith. You're not a mind reader."

"I should have noticed." Her fists clenched at her sides.

That's it. Get mad. Mad, she wouldn't look so vulnerable, wouldn't eat into the softening plate around his heart. "Beating yourself up isn't going to solve your problem."

"You're right." Her chin tilted up at a stubborn angle. "How do we figure out who this guy is?"

"First, we're going to take a drive to the closest hardware store."

"What for?"

"Your locks need changing."

She nodded. "I can call a locksmith to do it in the morning."

"You don't want *anyone* to have access to your new key."

"The building manager will need a copy, in case of emergency."

He shook his head. "Not until this stalker is behind bars."

She inhaled sharply. "Of course. You're right."

He hated bringing pain back into her eyes and suspicion back into her ordered life. She didn't need him. Not really. She just needed to regain confidence in her own strength. Just as he needed to keep on compartmentalizing.

Stick to the task. Give her the knowledge she needs to catch this creep.

Noah fought the rising mercury of temper. Emotions were going to get him nowhere. He had to get that through his thick skull. "Then I'm going to install a camera at each of the doors. If anyone tries to break in, he'll get caught on tape."

"And put an end to this nightmare."

He was used to handling problems, and he'd find the piece of scum eventually. But when Faith turned those pale blue eyes on him, the brilliant burning of trust in them shot him back twelve years, and nearly crumbled his resolve to keep his distance.

INSTEAD OF GOING through Faith's home computer, Noah spent a good chunk of the night dealing with the police, and purchasing then installing the new locks and cameras. With only a few hours of sleep under his belt, the next morning his eyes felt sandy, and his brain a bit fuzzy.

Noah downed the rest of his take-out coffee, hoping the caffeine would kick in before the department-head meeting started. He needed to study body language, all the subtle clues that gave away more than people thought. Faith had convinced him she was safe in her office while she gave Griffin a heads-up on their agreed-upon cover of Noah's being there to plug a security leak. She hated keeping her brother in the dark, but Noah wasn't ready to trust anyone with her welfare, not even family. He surveyed the paneled conference room with its oval teak table, dozen black leather chairs and fog-blanketed view of downtown. After choosing a corner seat that would give him a nonthreatening position, yet allow him to absorb the whole show, he took a detour to the men's room.

As he was washing his hands, Griffin entered. Noah gave him a nod in the mirror. Griffin's gaze narrowed like a hawk that'd spotted a mouse. Noah squared his shoulders. He might not have Falconer's height, Skyralov's linebacker shoulders or Mercer's fierce eyes, but he could hold his own.

"Griffin." Noah dried his hands and tossed the paper towel into the wastebasket.

Eyes crackling with hostility, Griffin blocked Noah's exit to the door. "It's not in your best interest to interfere with Byrne business. You have no idea what you're getting into."

"Computers happen to be my field of expertise."

"It's *family* business. We don't need an outsider meddling with sensitive information."

"Someone's already screwing with your sensitive information. If a guy can harvest your customers' credit-card information or come off the street with a fake receipt and get a refund for a purchase he never made, your bottom line's at stake."

Griffin's gaze narrowed. "I know who you are."

"Then you know I *am* good at what I do."

"You're the one who debauched Faith."

Debauched? That old-fashioned word could only come from uptight Philip Byrne. Who did Griffin think he was, passing judgment on something he knew nothing about? What Noah and Faith had shared that summer had been the closest thing to heaven he'd come across. But antagonizing Faith's stepbrother wasn't going to help her. This wasn't about him or Griffin or Philip Byrne. Noah had to keep his personal issues out of play. If Griffin had any idea that he could rattle him, Noah couldn't get his job done. Finding Faith's stalker was his only priority.

Noah's fingers curled into his palms. "I have Faith's best interests at heart."

"If you hurt her again, you'll have to answer to me."

Hurt her? He was the one who'd gotten skinned alive. The silence she'd meant as protection had cost him not only her, but his job and his reputation. For a while the threat of prison had even hung over his head, but his father's cool-headed lawyers had trumped Philip Byrne's rabid attorneys, and Noah had hung on to his freedom. "We were kids. I'm here to do a job, not pick up where we left off twelve years ago."

Griffin encroached into Noah's personal bubble. "See that your job is your solitary objective. You'll find I'm not as soft as Faith's father."

Noah leaned forward, meeting pressure with pressure. "And you'll find that I'm not easily intimidated."

"Faith belongs here, not in some back-woods town wasting her talent." The smoldering glare of Griffin's silver eyes was meant as a warning. "You have more to lose than some dinky camp job."

"I'm not worried."

"You should be." Without another word, Griffin turned on his heel and left.

Twelve years ago, Noah hadn't had the skills or the knowledge to help Faith. This time he had both. This time, no one was going to bulldoze her.

Not a stalker.
Not her family.

SERGIO SANDOZ, Faith's assistant, knocked and then popped his dark, curly head into her office. "Everybody's in the conference room waiting for you."

"Thanks, Sergio. I'll be right there."

Sergio wormed the rest of his skinny body in and placed a take-out cup of yogurt, fruit and granola from the café on her desk.

"I've told you before," Faith said, gathering her notes. "You don't have to fetch things for me."

His bright eyes took her in and one corner of his mouth lifted in delight. "Ah, but *mija,* you cannot go into that meeting with an empty stomach. Passing out is not the impression you want to make on all those *perros hambrientos.*"

Hungry dogs—that about covered the way they would all react to her when she walked in. "You're right. Thanks."

Sergio handed her a stack of messages, then went back to his post.

Faith leafed through the messages, separating them as she went. Usually the thought of a full conference room brought her pleasure, a sense of purpose. Not today. Her father expected her to have a spine of steel, to present an authoritative front to their employees. How would he feel knowing one of them wanted his daughter dead? He'd probably blame her, say she'd asked for it somehow with her weak managerial skills.

She looked at the yogurt cup. Her stomach rebelled. She ignored the food as she gathered her notes.

"Everything okay?" Sergio asked as she strode by his desk.

"I'm fine." What she needed to concentrate on was the task ahead: the department-head meeting she had to conduct in a few minutes so that Noah could uncover who was trying to break her.

She paused before the conference room, straightened the hem of the gray suit jacket from Byrne's own private label, then entered the room buzzing with people, and caught Noah's eye.

His intense gaze and the quick quirk of his smile, just for her, flooded her system with feel-good warmth that had her relaxing in a way she hadn't in a long, long time. And then the relaxation turned the curve into something else, something hotter, something hungry, making her feel like that nervous sixteen-year-old on Blueberry Island all those summers ago, expectant, eager, scared to death.

Controlled energy. That was the one thing she remembered much too vividly about Noah.

And that controlled energy was what she needed to emulate now. She couldn't get tangled up in the mess of her emotions. She had to put up a good front before her employees, let them know that she was unequivocally in control.

In her best take-charge voice, Faith introduced Noah as a computer security expert, hired to make the store's electronic network safer from the rash of fraud befalling the store lately. Naturally Kit Gadwah, the IT manager, wasn't pleased with this outside interference into "his" territory.

"Have I done something to offend you, Miss Byrne?" Kit's Indian-accented voice lilted softly from across the room. His normally warm brown eyes chilled to coal.

"No, Kit. You're doing a terrific job. I need

you to get together with Receiving and to put all of your energy into making sure all the bugs are worked out of the new inventory tracking system by the end of the week. The changeover is bound to stir up chaos. Mr. Kingsley's expertise is in computer security. He'll run an analysis of our system and give us some ideas to improve our anti-theft protocols. Turning those suggestions into reality will be your job."

"Have I not kept the system operating efficiently?"

"You have, Kit. At this time of the year, though, we can all use extra help. We need to have a plan ready to execute before returns season hits. That's when we'll be at our most vulnerable. I would really appreciate your cooperation on this matter."

"Very well." But the grim set of Kit's mouth told her his cooperation was grudging.

"I would like all of you to cooperate and answer Mr. Kingsley's questions openly and honestly. It's for the good of the store. All of our livelihoods are at risk if we don't figure out how to curb theft."

There were a dozen people around the table. Any one of them could be her stalker.

All but Noah and Griffin. She hated keeping the stalker issue from her brother, but Noah had convinced her that, for now, it was best to keep her situation a secret.

Noah's gaze kept bouncing back to hers as if he were studying her subtle reactions to the others in the room. And every time he looked at her, her confidence shored up a notch.

Questions finally over, the meeting ended. Lying didn't come easily to her. The brave front she'd put on was just that—a front. As people left, her energy deflated as fast as if she were a tire with a puncture.

"I'll be heading down to IT with Mr. Gadwah," Noah said. "Where can I find you, if I need you?"

"I'll be in my office."

Stay there, his eyes said.

There was something infinitely comforting about knowing Noah had her back.

Griffin caught up to Faith in her office.

He dropped into Faith's leather swivel chair, pumped up to give her height when visitors came. He let go of his briefcase, propped up his elbows on the padded arms and tented his fingers above his lap. "Who is this guy?"

Noah. She'd sensed Griffin's obsession

with Noah last night at the restaurant and this morning when she'd told him she'd hired her old friend as a consultant. Ever since the disaster with Heath two years ago, her brother's overprotectiveness had pushed the edge into meddling, and no reminding him that she wasn't a teenager in need of a big brother's interference anymore seemed to help. He needed to learn to stay out of her personal life.

"I told you." Faith deftly closed the open file folders lying on her desk and piled them into her in-basket. In spite of the growing rift between them since he'd started working for Byrne's five years ago, she didn't feel comfortable with lying to him. "I hired Noah to look at our online security system. Fraudulent returns are at an all-time high, and we've had complaints about customer information getting into the wrong hands, so I'm being proactive. As Daddy is so fond of saying, proper preparation prevents poor performance."

"Why haven't I heard about this problem?"

"IT isn't your department."

"It's not yours, either. I deal with finances. Anything that affects money is my problem."

"I'm acting president right now, not just general manager." Though she hated to remind Griffin of her higher position within the company, she couldn't let him browbeat her. "Noah is a security specialist. He deals with this sort of thing all the time."

"I did some research, and I can't find much on him."

"Look, you can dig all you want, Griff, but there isn't anything fishy about him." She didn't want to deal with defending her decisions right now. Why did Griffin and her father insist on making her feel as if her judgment was lacking? "The only skeleton in Noah's closet is me."

"You? That incident at camp was his fault, not yours."

She brushed her brother away like the annoying gnat he was becoming. *He cares,* she reminded herself. "Never mind. It's old history."

"So you're throwing him a bone or something."

"No need. Noah's good at what he does. I need him. I trust him."

"Are you saying you don't trust me?"

She let out an exasperated sigh. Griffin

was so sensitive to perceived criticism, always had been. "No, that's not what I'm saying at all. I wanted an outside, independent eye to look at this problem before it became too big. Noah was available. Problem solved."

Griffin rose and grasped Faith's wrists. "We're in this together, Faith. We're family. Byrne's problems are our problems."

"I know." She twisted out of the shackle-like grip. "That's why I told you about Noah before the meeting."

And God knows her father would not approve of her course of action, either. Her story of hacker intrusion and theft-deterrent concerns to allow Noah access to find her stalker would not go over well. Never mind that she was trying to save the sacred public image her father insisted they maintain at all times rather than shouting her personal problems from the rooftops.

Faith sighed, falling back on the propriety Philip Byrne had drummed into both her and Griffin. "You want the best for Byrne's, don't you?"

"Of course." Picking up his briefcase, Griffin rose.

"Then Noah is it."

A charged beat elapsed as Griffin searched her eyes. "I expect full reports."

"Naturally." Family wasn't supposed to be at odds like this. "I'll keep you in the loop."

"Listen…" Griffin leaned in toward her and his voice deepened with a serious note. "There's something else I wanted to talk to you about."

"What?"

He placed his briefcase on the corner of her glass desk, then glowered at the door and closed it before snapping open the clasps and digging out a sheet of paper. "This."

His hand seemed reluctant to pass the sheet over. "I Google our names on a regular basis just to see what's floating out in cyberspace and keep on top of rumors. This is what I found last night."

Before or after you Googled Noah? On the piece of paper she took from him was a full-blown color picture of a blond woman caught in a provocative pose on a Pepto-Bismol–pink bed, her chest spilling over the low-cut neckline of a too-tight lacy black camisole, leaving nothing to the imagination. "What is this, and why are you showing it to me?"

"This is what popped up under your name."

She crammed the sheet back in his hand. "That's not me!"

"I know that, but no one else will. Look at it." He jammed the sheet under her nose.

"That doesn't look like me at all."

"It looks like someone used Photoshop to put your head over a model's body. It's your face, Faith. Remember the picture from the charity ball?"

Now that Griffin pointed it out, she could see the resemblance. She hated those events and had stayed only long enough to present Byrne's donation check, then had tried to slip away. A photographer had caught an expression of sheer relief as she'd made her escape into a taxi. And of course, that was the picture the *Seattle Times* had chosen to print. "Heiress on the Run," the headline covering the event had read.

"It was posted on a local chat room," Griffin said. "Turn the page and you'll see a listing of what you're willing to do for fifty dollars."

The text was so graphic, it made her empty stomach curdle. "How…"

"I don't know, but don't worry. I had the site owner take down the page."

That was a relief. He might be competing for her father's acceptance, but he was still looking after her, too. She should cut him some slack. "Thank you."

Her cell phone beeped. Thinking it was Noah, Faith flipped it open. A text message flashed on the screen and all heat drained out of her face. "i dont like the suit u r wearing. u shouldv worn the blue 1."

"What's wrong?"

She snapped the phone closed and dropped it on the desk as if it were too hot to handle. "Nothing. Look, I have to go down to IT. We'll talk about this later. Noah's not a threat. He's a friend. And he's here to help us, to help Byrne's."

"I'm here for you, too. You know that."

"Of course." She crossed to the door and held it open. "The best thing you can do for me right now is make sure that Jaworski gets on board with the inventory control system he was supposed to have started using in September. He'll listen to you. With Dad sick, that would be a huge worry off my plate."

"No problem."

She touched his forearm in a show of solidarity. "It's good to know I can depend on you, Griffin."

His smile held no warmth. With her father sick, he had as much to prove as she did. And when her father came back and tallied the points, Griffin could very well end up with the bigger share. It shouldn't matter. He was family.

But it mattered.

A lot.

Her grandfather had started Byrne's. Her grandmother had kept it going after her grandfather's early death and grown the business to a reckoning force in Seattle. Her father had nearly run the whole thing into the ground before Griffin's mother had come along and given Byrne's a much-needed cash injection.

Faith had poured her sweat and soul into turning Byrne's around. She wasn't going to let Griffin take credit for all of her effort. He would have to earn his position at Byrne's—just as she had.

She wasn't going to let a stalker take her life's work away from her, either, or use him as an excuse to let Griffin walk away with what was hers.

As Faith rested her forehead against the

closed door, her cell phone warbled again. With shaking fingers, she reached for it, hoping, praying the message was from Noah.

It wasn't.

"how strong r u?" the message read. "i m going 2 test u."

Chapter Four

Faith lay in her bed, staring at the lights rippling shadows across her ceiling like water. The ebb and flow of traffic on the streets below, usually soothing, now droned like a crazed mosquito.

She couldn't sleep. Her mind kept replaying the text messages her stalker had sent her. *I'm going to test you.*

How? When? *Why?*

After Griffin had left her office, she'd hightailed it to IT where Noah was sitting with Kit, getting a tour of Byrne's system. Noah had pulled a few of his Seekers strings and traced the text messages she'd received to one of those cell phones paid for in cash. Real owner unknown.

Of course.

She turned to her side and ground her head

into the pillow. What had she said or done to move someone to taunt her this way? She'd worked hard to do everything right.

The worst part of this situation was not knowing *who*. Without that tidbit of information, stopping him seemed impossible.

Ever since her grandmother had taken her to afternoon tea at Byrne's newly-opened café when Faith was nine, Faith had known she'd wanted the respect and esteem her grandmother had garnered as she'd walked through the store. She'd never thought of doing anything except one day running Byrne's. Through tea and scones, her grandmother had explained her philosophy regarding the shopping experience. "Give the customer what she wants," her grandmother had said, "and she'll come back again and again."

Even at that young age, Faith had understood the flip side of the coin. If the customer didn't like her experience, she would go elsewhere.

"One day this will all be yours," Gran had said as they'd left the store, and her blue eyes had glittered. "I know you'll make me proud."

Faith remembered how fiercely she'd wanted to please her grandmother, make

Gran's eyes shine for her as brightly as they had for the store.

Now this stalker was stripping away her confidence bit by bit. According to the research she'd done that afternoon, murder was the leading cause of death for American women in the workplace, and the wearing down of defenses was the number-one tool in a stalker's bag of tricks.

Unable to stay still, she got up and went to the window. From her darkened room, she nudged the Roman shade aside and examined the surrounding buildings to see if she could spot someone watching her.

This was crazy. She let go of the shade and turned back to her bed. Just because her stalker was jerking strings didn't mean she had to react the way he wanted. She wouldn't let him see that she was scared. She wouldn't give him the attention he craved. She would keep running her business as if he didn't exist.

She wasn't alone. She had Noah.

Just as she lifted the comforter, a muffled thud caught her attention.

Noah? She'd reluctantly left him tinkering with her computer. He'd insisted she go to bed, that one of them should be rested.

But rest was impossible. Understanding what he was doing to find her stalker would jack up her confidence, and with confidence, she could defeat this parasite.

Faith picked up a pink silk bathrobe from the chair at the vanity and slipped it on. She could keep up the proper boundaries. The lessons of propriety her father had drilled in her head made her good at keeping up appearances.

She frowned at the darkness greeting her outside her bedroom. If Noah was working, shouldn't the desk light be on?

Pale fingers of light filtered through the gauzy sheers of her living room and her eyes, already adjusted to the night, took in the lumpy shapes of the couch, two club chairs and the chinoiserie table. The rounded forms of the cobalt-blue glass bottles on the vintage end tables reflected the outside lights like yellow cat eyes.

At a noise, which sounded like a dog scratching at the door, she swiveled her head toward the kitchen. But as soon as she thought she'd found its origin, it stopped. Had she imagined it because her mind was on the stalker?

The eerie ticks of her grandmother's clock

sent her thoughts racing down the track of all the horrible things that could have already happened. The stalker had gotten in again. He'd hurt Noah. Noah was out there in the dark, bleeding to death while she stood there frozen.

She glanced back at the hallway that led to her bedroom and the guest bedroom. She tried calling out to Noah, but all that clambered up her throat was a dry croak.

Do you hear yourself? You're sounding like the next victim in a slasher movie.

Noah had barely slept in two days. He was probably catching up on much-needed rest. She didn't want to wake him just because her imagination had gone wild, imprinting normal night noises with an excess of drama.

She focused on her breaths, chugging out too fast to the runaway rhythm of her heart, but couldn't quite slow either down.

She'd make a mug of chamomile tea. That would ease her back to sleep. In the morning she'd have to deal with spring advertising and fall merchandising and review the retail identity tweaks she planned on implementing throughout the coming year, not to mention the day-to-day problems that were bound to crop up. She needed sleep, too.

She was reaching for a mug in the cupboard when the noise came again. A *scritch-scritch* at the door that led to the emergency stairway.

Someone was trying to get in.

For endless seconds she stood there, hoping to blend into the shadows, hoping the intruder would miss her in the dark, knowing full well that the first flip of a light switch would spotlight her.

She opened her mouth to call Noah, but no sound came out. *Find him. Wake him.*

Muscles tensed. A rush of heat flooded her veins, and her brain fired a splintering jumble of thoughts. Focus. Why couldn't she focus?

Heart still beating a throb of warning, she willed her knees to unlock, willed her thoughts to a hush, willed the intruder away. With excruciating care, she placed one bare foot in front of the other, heading for Noah's bedroom.

As she neared the kitchen island, the phone rang. She let out a small yelp and reached to quell the shrill ringing. "Hello?"

"My love for you is undying," the raspy voice said. It could've been anyone, but the hard slam of her heart against her ribs knew it was him. Her stalker. The man who was turning her life into a theater of terror. "I'll wait for you my whole life. But I won't share you with him. Don't ignore me. Make him go away."

The click of the him hanging up came before she'd quite regained her composure.

"Faith?"

Gasping, she whirled to face the whisper in the dark, and found Noah behind her, looking like some sort of fantasy come to life with his unbuttoned jeans, stubble-shadowed jaw and intense eyes. "Oh, God, Noah, you took a year off my life."

The ebbing tide of adrenaline left her shaky, and her head sank onto his chest, caught the sharp intake of his breath. He ran a hand over her hair, keeping her safe in the solid circle of his arms. She drank in the pulse of his warmth, and her strung-up muscles started to unwind.

"Who was on the phone?" he asked, voice low and soothing.

She shook her head against his heated skin, wanted to fold herself right into him. "I don't know. But he doesn't like you. He ordered me to make you go away."

"He won't chase me off. I promise."

That promise kicked in a new kind of terror. She'd brought Noah here. She was responsible for him. What if he got hurt because of her? She'd already allowed him to suffer because of her once. Her hands gripped his shoulders. "I don't think it's safe for you here."

"He's picking on the wrong guy." Noah's lips kicked up against her skull. "I eat scum like him for breakfast every day."

He was trying to make light of the stalker's threat, but she couldn't let go of the feeling that she'd put him in danger's path. If anything happened to him, she would never forgive herself. "What if—"

"Not negotiable," Noah said into her hair, lulling her into believing he could do anything. "I'm staying." As if to make his point, he segued back to the business of the call. "A trace'll probably lead us to another disposable phone, but I'll run it in the morning."

He gently nudged her out of his arms. "Why are you walking around in the dark?"

Away from Noah's heat, her body shivered. His magnetic pull still drew at her, and the weak side of her wanted him close again, wanted to lean on him—and not just to catch her stalker. But he was her friend, and she couldn't risk losing that by giving in to old memories. Warming her arms with a quick rub of her hands, she gave an unruffled shrug. "I thought I heard a noise."

And there it was again, a determined clash of metal against metal at the emergency door.

Noah's body coiled like a predator on alert. With his cell phone, he called the police, speaking their language. His usually ready smile and laid-back manner made it easy to forget he was a trained agent. But this transformation into efficient protector calmed her ragged nerves in a way she didn't want to admit.

"When I give you the signal," he whispered, holstering his cell phone into his back pocket, "turn on the lights."

He was sending her to the other side of the room, she realized, out of harm's way. "Wait for the police."

"If he's going to make it in before they get here," he whispered back, "I want it to be on our terms."

Noah silently made his way to the door in the kitchen alcove. He positioned himself flat on the wall by the door, listening to the intruder's scratching. Without making a noise, he slid the dead bolt from its hole, then reached for the latch. Fingers securely in place, he gave one hard nod.

He released the lock and sprang the door open. Faith snapped on the overhead light. The masked intruder, dressed in black from head to toe, was taken by surprise and froze. Using the intruder's momentary rooted state, Noah flipped the man to the ground, knocking the wind out of him. But before Noah could cuff him with the handcuffs dangling from the man's tight black leather pants, the intruder was on his feet again, fists aimed at Noah's face.

Fast. Everything was happening too fast. Noah and the intruder scuffled in a blur. Noah was going to get hurt.

Faith didn't think, she just moved. She reached into the cupboard for the never-used Calphalon skillet. Holding the skillet two-handed like a tennis racket, she aimed it at the intruder. The blow to his upper back— she couldn't quite reach his head—dropped him to a knee, slowing him down.

As the intruder turned toward her, Noah

wrestled him to the ground and shackled him with the handcuffs. "Got some rope?"

Faith scrounged through her junk drawer, but all she could come up with was an extension cord. "Will this do?"

Noah bound the man's ankles with the extension cord, then ripped off his black mask and turned to Faith. "Do you know him?"

He looked like Mr. Clean's evil twin with his onyx eyes, ripped shoulders and skintight black leather jacket and pants. She shook her head and the noodly-rubber feeling returned to her legs. "I've never seen him in my life."

"Got a name?" Noah asked.

Eyes bulging from his bald head, the man blinked rapidly as if sorting through all of his possible options.

"Not a talker, huh?" Noah rammed the much bigger man against the wall, propping him into a sitting position. "No problem. The cops'll be here any second now."

"Cops?" The man's bound feet scrambled beneath him as he tried to stand. "Hey, that wasn't part of the game."

Noah shoved him back into place. "Game? What game?"

"The *game*." His narrowed gaze turned on

Faith. "You asked for this. Said you wanted to be scared."

Hand over her knocking heart, Faith backed away. He'd achieved his goal; she was petrified. "I didn't—"

"Ah, come on, honey. You can't change your mind. That's not fair. I played by the rules. I came after midnight, just like you said. I wore the frigging mask, just like you wanted." He jiggled his captive wrists. "I even brought real handcuffs."

"Where did you get all this *information?*" Noah asked.

The man eyed Noah as if he were a poor sap. "From the sex-fantasy chat room. She said hers was rape." He took vicious pleasure at spitting out the words as if they were darts and Noah's ego was the target. "That she'd pay for a good scare."

Faith sucked in a breath. Who would do something so cruel as to set her up this way?

"And you volunteered, just like that, to fulfill her dark fantasy?"

One side of the man's mouth curled like a snarling dog. "She picked me. Gave her address, told me where she'd left the key, and how to bypass her home security system."

His voice exploded with indignation. "I don't do this for kicks, you know. I need the money."

"How much?" The barely controlled rumble in Noah's voice scared even her.

"She messengered me a thousand bucks. Said she'd double it if I came tonight. Give an extra bonus if I made her scream."

Oh, God, how could this be happening? How had she gotten caught in this nightmare? When would it end?

She jumped at the pounding at the front door. "Seattle police!"

But even as she scrambled to open the door for the police, Faith knew this man's capture wasn't the end of her ordeal. Like her, he was merely a pawn.

ENSCONCED IN A CORNER of Faith's office at the round table she'd cleared for him, Noah had watched Faith all day, calling himself a fool on at least a dozen counts. He couldn't seem to let her out of his sight.

The fact she was bothering him was his problem, not hers, and he needed to get over it.

He turned back to the three computers on the table. He'd bit-imaged the hard drives from her home computer last night and had done the same to her office computer when he came in that morning. The proprietary forensics programs even the best labs didn't yet have access to were running through their paces, deciphering all of the hard drives' secrets. Getting answers was more a matter of time than attention.

Faith needed progress.

The smarting pain of his jaw from the punk's fist was a reminder that protecting her and finding the stalker were his only objectives. He had to remember that. But last night's break-in was a chicken-or-egg conundrum. If his presence at Faith's apartment hadn't made the stalker jealous, would he have set her up on the sex chat room? But if he hadn't been there, and the stalker had set her up anyway, then that chat room creep would have harmed her.

Threat or no from the stalker, Noah wouldn't leave Faith to face the menace alone. He had to get her out of here—out of the store, out of her condo, out of Seattle.

And he knew how well that suggestion was going to go over.

The progress bar signaled completion on

Faith's home computer. Noah read through the reports, not liking what he was finding.

He put his glasses back on, and brought Faith, hard at work behind her behemoth chrome-and-glass desk, into focus.

Since the store's opening at ten, she'd received calls, e-mails and visits from strange men wanting to fulfill her fantasies— not that any of those had made it past the security Noah insisted guard the elevator at her floor after the first one had gotten past Sergio around ten-thirty. Little by little, he could see the edge of her protective wall fray, the border of her determination shrivel. As much as she wanted to keep up a competent front, she was falling apart.

Her pain pressed against him, wearing down his intention to stay indifferent.

He had to get her out of town.

She caught him looking at her and gave him a small smile, holding herself tall and proud, trying to mask the unending chain of her torment. All that upper-crust stiffness gave her an unapproachable look—until he glanced at her lips, ripe with sensuality, filling him with a terrible hunger that had gone unsated too long.

"Anything?" Faith asked from behind the barrier of her desk, desperation leaking through her voice. She was alone in a world that should be hers to command.

When he didn't answer, she nudged her chin in his computer's direction.

"Whoever this guy is…" Noah leaned back in the well-oiled chair as if he hadn't a care in the world. "…he knows how to cover his steps."

"Aren't criminals supposed to be dumb?"

"That's what I count on." He kept his tone a little mocking, a little teasing. Best way for him to keep his head on straight.

"But not this guy." Her sadness scored his heart.

Reluctantly, he shared the bad news his preliminary results had yielded. "The e-mails the stalker sent you were routed through anonymous remailers."

"Which means?"

"They'll be hard to trace."

"I thought you said everything leaves footprints."

"It does. These messages are chained, meaning each message was sent through a series of different anonymizing e-mail servers. Each server that a message passes through adds another layer of security, making it harder to ID the real source of the e-mail. Once it's gone through four or more servers it's practically impossible to trace. I'm not giving up, but…"

Though she kept her hands in her lap and her feet grounded on the floor, her inner growl of frustration reverberated in his skull.

"He wins again," she said.

"Not necessarily. He made one mistake."

"What?" she breathed, as if afraid to get her hopes up.

"There's a key logger on your home computer. And I'm betting there's one on your office computer, too."

"What's that?"

"It's a program that monitors all the activity on your computer. Every time you hit a key, it's saved and sent to whoever installed the surveillance software. With that he has access to everything you typed, including passwords."

"Can you find out where it's going?"

He slanted her a sly smile. "I'll set up a firewall to catch where the information is being sent. When the report goes out tonight,

I'll get an address back. I'll add a bonus piggyback program onto his and see what I can scout out."

The pen in Faith's hand twirled, mirroring the gymnastics of her mind processing the information. "What about the other stuff?"

Noah scrubbed his hair. "I tracked the GPS serial number to an online store. A man who's been dead for three years bought it."

Her eyebrows shot up. "Identity theft?"

"Looks that way. I had a local P.I. outfit track the orchids. They came from a stand at the Pike Place Market. Cash is common there, and the woman couldn't remember if anyone had bought just three orchids. Seems they were a special buy, and she sold a lot of them this week."

"And the bullets?"

A hive of frustration buzzed in his gut. "My guy didn't get anything off them. They were fresh out of the box, so there were no markings on them." And if the stalker was smart, they wouldn't match any of the weapons he owned. The police lab would be much slower in getting results from the paper birds and other evidence they'd collected from Faith's condo. Her case wasn't a priority. Not until she got hurt. And he wasn't going to let it get to that point.

Faith dropped the pen. "He's like a ghost. Invisible and one step ahead."

"We'll catch him," he said, and ground his back teeth.

She sighed. "I just wish it was sooner rather than later."

Me, too. "Background checks are trickling in. Nothing's standing out so far, except maybe your neighbor, Max Hessel. What do you know about him?"

She shrugged. "Not much. His father built the building where I live. He works in real estate—when he works. What did you find?"

"A financial mess." And a weakness for porn. With Hessel's father owning the building, did he have access to Faith's condo keys and her alarm code?

"That's surprising. He's always throwing money around as if it means nothing to him."

Which was probably how he'd gotten in trouble. "Has he ever asked you out?"

She brushed away his question with a flap of her hand. "A couple of times. But I think it was more of a hey-I-don't-want-you-to-feel-left-out type of thing. He's got a new date every night. He doesn't have to resort to stalking to get a woman's attention."

Maybe. Maybe not. Wouldn't hurt to have Falconer's local P.I. contact follow Hessel.

Noah rose and skirted Faith's desk. He twirled her jacked-up chair until she faced him and crouched beside her. "I'm worried about you."

"I'm fine, really. Just frustrated."

She tried to swivel back to her desk, but he held firm. "The stalker's obsession with you seems to be accelerating."

She swallowed hard, but shored up that damned Byrne everything's-okay front. "That means he'll make a mistake, and we'll be able to get him."

"I'm not willing to take that risk. I know a place where we can go—"

She leaned forward, palms pressing hard against the chair's arms, and gave him a stare as cold and keen as any Philip Byrne could conjure up. "I can't leave."

Noah's hands itched to shake reason into her, but that fell into the category of "bad idea" for both of them. Especially when they were this close and all he had to do was bend his head to kiss her. "Are you waiting until he hurts you to get some sense?"

She flinched, then turned those pale blue eyes on him and silently begged for understanding. "It feels like giving up."

Damn those eyes. He couldn't let them get to him. "It's survival."

She broke his hold and looked away, busying herself with the mess of papers on her desk. "I have to be back by Sunday afternoon."

"One day isn't going to give me much of a chance to do anything to corner him." As he stood, he recognized the stubborn streak frosting every inch of her. Like his sisters, she'd had that high-and-mighty skill down even at sixteen. Nothing was going to move her—except maybe her father's ire, and Philip Byrne was conveniently unavailable.

"It's Byrne's employee holiday party," she said. "With Dad in the hospital, it's my obligation to put in an appearance."

"Griffin—"

"Is my brother, but he's not a Byrne. I can't disappoint my employees. They expect me to show up."

"They'll understand."

She tilted her head and slanted him a sweet smile laced with sadness. "Hiding the truth was your idea."

Yes, it was. And he still believed in that decision. He'd accept her compromise, for now. Once he had her on the island, he'd find a way to keep her there. "It'll take me half an hour to round up my equipment."

She glanced at the work spread over her desk. "It's only three. I have a lot more work to do before I can leave."

"The sooner I find him, the sooner you can get back to your killer schedule."

She nodded and reached for her briefcase.

They worked side by side in silence until she was ready to go. The stony silence dragged behind them like leg irons, followed them down the elevator, through the colorful displays of women's sweaters, skirts and dresses that made up the main aisle of Byrne's retail floor, all the way out to the dismal gray of the parking lot and Faith's car. Holiday flags snapped against metal poles. Rain fell from a swirling mass of clouds, drops plinking against the car's hood like sharpened nails.

A bright yellow piece of paper, trapped by

the windshield wiper, flapped in the rain-heavy breeze. His first instinct was to put himself between Faith and trouble, but in this wide-open space, it could attack them from all directions.

They would have to rent a car. Hers was too much of a beacon. He handed her his phone. "Call the cops."

With tweezers from the penknife he carried in his pocket, Noah extricated the note.

"You don't seem to appreciate my efforts," the note read, "so I'm changing the rules."

HE'D WARNED HER. He'd warned him. White-hot rage built to a boil in his chest. After all he'd done for her. After all he'd sacrificed to ensure their future. How could she betray him like this?

It was all right. He was still in control. He knew exactly what to do. She wasn't leaving him any choice.

He needed to show her his pain. He needed to make her understand what she'd done to him.

If she didn't send the hotshot away, he would have to.

Chapter Five

Faith hung on to the sides of the motorboat with both hands, the cold spray of water a bracing reminder to stay in the present and not let her mind plunge her into the world of what-ifs. That was kind of hard to do, though, with the present and the past blurring along with the landscape.

They were heading to Lovan Island, a sixteen-acre private island near Gig Harbor. Only minutes away by boat, but far enough that it seemed on the other side of the moon. A sad sky shed tears and the weight of all those what-ifs was a stone in her heart.

Did Noah realize what he was doing by taking her there? To an island? Just as he had twelve years ago?

At sixteen, her head full of romance, she'd talked him into borrowing a canoe and going out for a ride after their respective camps were asleep. She'd put together a picnic from items acquired from the mess hall at camp. They were going to be alone, without all the other Boy Scouts and pampered princesses watching them like a sideshow for their entertainment. They hadn't planned on what happened—not really—it just had, and with the stars and the moon and the blanket—somehow she never remembered the mosquitoes—merging into each other's arms, into each other's bodies, had felt so right and good.

Until the search parties had found them naked and asleep the next morning, and turned their secret getaway into a mortifying embarrassment. And somehow poor Noah had ended up painted as a predator when all along she was the one who'd teased him right out of his khaki shorts…

"What if—" Noah stammered after their illicit picnic when she'd rejected his suggestion they head back to camp.

She'd thrown her head back and laughed. "What if the moon drops out of the sky? What if the world stops turning? What if we never get another chance? Don't you like me, Noah? Not even a little?"

"You don't know what you do to me." The hunger so raw and open in his eyes had turned her wicked.

She'd smiled at him, all hormones and temptation, wound her arms around his neck, pressed her half-naked body against his and reveled in the tremor down the length of his as she'd brought her lips to hover close to his. "Then kiss me."

And that hungry kiss had rocked her world.

She'd never stopped loving Noah, but she'd understood long ago that a relationship with him wouldn't work. At least she thought she had. They wanted different things out of life, and she couldn't ask him to give up his dreams any more than she could leave hers behind. Most of all, she couldn't have stood to see the love in his eyes turn to resentment over the years, or worse, hatred.

But that island…it made her want to find the girl who wasn't scared to ask for what she wanted, consequences be damned.

Noah slowed the boat. The wet breeze blew a strand of hair out of her eyes, opening up scenery from a dream. All this water and trees and privacy had to weigh on Noah's mind, too. Why else would he be chattering on like some tour guide?

"This island used to have four houses, but my college roommate, Ben Lovan—who leans on the eccentric side—bought them up with his software earnings so he could have a private retreat. He mowed down all the homes, then designed and built a new one."

Noah guided the boat into the slip and killed the engine. After tying up the boat, he offered her a hand.

Towering firs surrounded the storybook Tudor home with its shake-shingle roof and brown brick facade. Enough clearing remained for breathtaking views of the sound and, no doubt, glorious sunrises over Mount Rainier.

As if to dislodge the tightness stringing his voice and body, Noah hefted all of the bags out of the boat and loaded them onto his broad shoulders.

"I can carry something." She reached out and grabbed her overnight bag and briefcase, much too aware of the tension between them primed to spark.

As if they were expected, a welcoming light shone from sconces at each side of the front door. "Is your friend there?"

"No, he's in Europe and won't be back for a couple of weeks."

Through the trees, framed by afternoon sky darkening to night, she spied a gazebo with a hot tub, a fire pit and a swimming pool.

Everything one could desire to create a serene and quiet haven. Just what they both needed right now. Except for all the childhood fantasies she couldn't chase out of her wistful skull. Hot tubs and fire pits weren't helping the situation.

Noah's friend was indeed eccentric—at least when it came to decorating. The whole house was decked out in shades of brown, every room stocked with dark, massive, manly furniture.

Noah took his bag of gadgets to Ben's computer room, which was like a home office on steroids. Computers, monitors, electronic gizmos and doodads of all kind furnished the room more fully than a Microsoft lab. No wonder Noah had been able to travel light. He plugged wires and pushed buttons and made the whole operation look as graceful as a conductor leading an orchestra.

Once everything hummed, Noah moved his

restless energy to the kitchen where he pulled packages of rice pilaf, turkey cutlets and frozen green beans from Ben's well-stocked freezer and whipped them into a meal.

Faith found silverware and napkins while Noah set their steaming plates onto the marble-topped kitchen island.

Digging in as if he hadn't eaten all day, Noah asked, "How was your father?"

After the police had come to retrieve the stalker's latest love letter, they'd rented a car and stopped at the hospital to see her father. Well, she had. Noah had stayed downstairs, pacing the waiting room. She couldn't blame him. Not after the way her father had treated him. Not after the way she'd taken the coward's way out and hadn't stood up for him.

"He opened his eyes, but I don't think he knew who I was." The renewed hurt ruined what little appetite she had, and she picked at the orzo-and-rice pilaf. "I wish the doctors knew what was wrong with him."

"I thought you said he'd had a heart attack."

"They thought maybe he'd had a stroke at the same time, but all the tests came back negative. They can't figure out why he's being so unresponsive."

"He's been working hard for decades. Maybe it's his body's way of telling him to take a break."

"Maybe." What if he died? She shook her head and cut the turkey cutlet into smaller and smaller pieces with the edge of her fork. She wasn't going to go down that road. He wasn't going to die. He couldn't. Not before…

Before what? You make him proud? You're not six or ten or even sixteen anymore. What he thinks doesn't matter.

She pushed her barely touched plate away. "So what happens next?"

Noah put his plate in the sink and, with a raise of one eyebrow, asked if she was done with hers. She nodded and handed it to him.

"Next…" Noah leaned across the counter and looked straight into her eyes. The soothing pinwheels of brown and green calmed her sandblasted nerves. "I'm going to go check on the computers."

Even though they'd told no one where they were going, she still had bad flashes of the throng of unsavory men who'd found their way to the store and feared they would somehow discover her hideaway, so she followed Noah to the computer room.

"What's with all this computer equipment?" she asked, seeking to distract herself from her useless fears. She perched on a stool and hovered close by, watching Noah's hands fly over the keyboard.

"Ben develops software, and he's not really into corporate life. He does his best work here."

"What kind of stuff does he do?"

"Corporate security mostly. But his real passion is forensics. His twin sister was murdered last year at MIT. They never found the guy. Ben and Sara had a special bond. He never forgave himself for being too drunk that night to hear her calls for help."

"That's horrible." Faith could empathize. The car and driver that had run her grandmother and Rhea, Griffin's mother, off the road five years ago, causing their deaths, had never been found either. She'd turned her anger at the lack of closure into renewed determination to make Byrne's a success for Gran. And now, another unknown person was trying to take away her strength. "This piggyback firewall thing you installed on my computers, it'll find whoever's keeping track of my every keystroke?"

"It'll give me an IP address."

One eyebrow shot up in question.

"His computer address."

With an address would come a name. An identity. An arrest.

Her pulse quickened. It was almost over. This nightmare was finally going to end.

Her life would soon go back to normal.

EVEN THROUGH THICK layers of sleep fogging his eyes, and his glasses off, Noah was aware of Faith standing at his bedroom door, one hand spread flat on the door, the other wrapped around the doorknob.

"Noah? Are you asleep?"

Amber light spilled from the bedside lamp, gilding her like an ethereal pixie. Through half-closed eyes, he could make out the drape of the extra-long, mint-green T-shirt she wore, sheathing her as sensually as a Roman toga. For a second he wondered if he was dreaming; he'd had that whimsical vision of her coming to him at night so many times before.

He should take the out she offered, pretend he was asleep, let the fantasy carry him to deeper slumber, but the note of terror in her voice roused every protective instinct in his body. "Are you all right?"

"I-I…" She came into the room, her footfalls almost silent on the thick carpet, and stopped at the foot of his bed, both hands gripping the sleigh bed's footboard as if she needed its support. "W-would you mind if I slept with you tonight?"

Panic leaped into his blood, and he scrambled to sitting. "You mean in this bed?"

Eyes wide like a frightened kitten, she nodded. "All the noises outside…I just…I just can't get those sex-crazed men who came to the store out of my head. Every time I close my eyes they're there with their monster's smiles and, and——" She shook her head in small, tight arcs. "I won't bother you. I promise. I just can't be alone right now."

Before his mind had time to itemize the reasons why her request wasn't a good idea, his arm flipped back the covers, allowing her into the warm folds of his bed. She snuggled in, turned her back to him, balancing her body on the edge of the queen-size mattress, careful not to let any part of her touch any part of him.

Not that it helped.

Her heat rippled like a desert mirage. The taut in and out of her breathing tugged at his pulse. The rose and sun-dried laundry scent of her was a cocktail of adrenaline, caffeine and amphetamine, designed to lure a man, make him leave his senses at the door, and fall straight into her many charms.

Oh, yeah, she bothered him all right. A head-to-toe bother. A bother of the mind. A bother of the senses. A bother of the… *Yeah, let's not go there.*

All he had to do was turn over and he could skim his hand along her narrow waist, dovetail his body along the curve of her spine, along all that smooth, soft skin beneath the thin material of her shirt.

He flexed a fist. He was there to solve a problem, not create one.

Trouble was, he liked having her around. It made him feel more alive somehow. All that tight energy wound in that small body was a jolt out of the ruts he tended to fall into. Or maybe it was because she was easy on the eyes. Yeah, those eyes. The blue so pale, he always thought he was looking into an endless cloud-filtered sky.

He was walking a tightrope, swaying way off balance. If he wasn't careful, he'd end up all broken again.

And that was definitely something he wanted to avoid. Boundaries were there for a reason. When the scum was skimmed, he'd go back to his life, and she'd go on with hers. Fashion and felons were a world apart. The two weren't meant to collide and mesh seamlessly.

But when it came to Faith, he'd never had much sense—common, horse or otherwise— and she was trying much too hard to hide her fears. He rolled onto his side, slid his arm over her waist and spooned her up against him. So much for calming down. Every inch of him throbbed as if his nerves were on fire. And need, deep and primal, rocked through him in a fierce craving.

"I'm okay," Faith said, her voice thick with tears. "You don't have to hold me."

I do. "I can't sleep with all that clacking of bones."

"I'll stop."

"Shh," he whispered in her hair, drinking in her sense-drugging scent. He could do this. He was twenty-nine, not seventeen. He could hold her as a friend. He could soothe her fears. "Just go to sleep."

In the frantic minutes he took to win the war of wills over his body, her tense muscles relaxed, and she fell asleep.

But none of the mental calisthenics he performed could keep his mind off the woman cocooned in his arms.

He had to collar that stalker. Before it was too late.

"I'VE GOT HIM!" Noah's shout the next morning when Faith was halfway through the stack of pancakes he'd left for her had her racing to the computer room. He pumped a fist in the air and flashed her a megawatt smile over his shoulder.

He'd saved her from embarrassment with her lack of propriety last night by getting up before dawn. Faith had thought about staying in bed all day with the covers pulled up over her head so she wouldn't have to deal with her cowardice. After all, Noah had shown her the state-of-the-art security system, how to arm and disarm each component. The show-and-tell was meant to demonstrate that, should anyone reach the island, they would not get into the house.

But the ceaseless rustle of night creatures, the eerie creaks of tree limbs and the greedy licks of water against the shore and rain against the roof had spooked her, and her wild imagination had finally driven her to the sanctuary of his bed. And she'd made a fool of herself, hanging on to him all night long as if he were the only life preserver in the vast ocean of her off-kilter world.

The scent of coffee and her growling stomach had finally lured her to the kitchen. After a shower, and dressed in a white blouse, deep V-neck gray cashmere sweater and skinny black pants, she almost felt like herself again.

"You found him?" She parked herself behind Noah's chair and looked over his shoulder, fingers brushing against the soft material of his sweater as she leaned on to the back of the chair. "Who? Where?"

He twirled his chair around to face her, triumph shining bright in his eyes. "I know from where he's been accessing your computer."

She sucked in a breath, folding her hands over her heart. "Where?"

"A place called On Line Coffee Company."

"That's downtown, not far from Byrne's." Hope brimmed. "So it's over?"

"Not quite."

But her relief was so great that his words of caution didn't faze her. "I knew you could do it."

She threw her arms around his neck and kissed him on the cheek. The next thing she knew, she'd lost her balance and was sitting in his lap. They sat eye to eye, unmoving, a warning glowing brightly in the swirls of green and brown of his gaze. Not wise to fall prey to temptation's lure, but he'd saved her, he'd found her stalker, he'd given her her life back, and pure gratefulness bubbled up from deep inside her. With slow, deliberate care, she lowered her mouth to his, giving him plenty of chance to refuse her token of thanks.

The first taste of him unraveled time, taking her back to that summer. She melted against him, fitting to him as perfectly as she had then. Her mind tumbled back into the soul-spinning vortex of fervent teenage desire. She opened to him, touching, tasting, needing.

He slid a hand into her hair, angling for a deeper exploration of her mouth. Awareness of him snapped and arced, tingling every one of her nerve endings. The heat he generated burned, blurring all logic from her mind, and she slid, fast, way too fast, down a very dangerous slope.

Only Noah had ever managed to trip her over the edge of insanity like this.

This—whatever it was—should have faded by now. She was a grown woman. She'd survived two serious relationships and a botched marriage without losing herself. She should be immune to Noah.

She made a move to push against his chest, but couldn't seem to put any force into her hand.

"Noah…" His name purred in her throat and a helpless feeling unfurled with breathless longing.

As if her weakness had sobered him, he leaned his forehead against hers, his breath not quite steady. "Ah, Faith. What are we doing?"

"I have no idea. But it's not…"

"Yeah, definitely not…"

"It would complicate things."

"Like last time," he agreed.

"It wasn't your fault."

"I know."

"My father—"

He touched a finger to her lips. "Shh. Let's not dredge up old history."

She nodded. "I just wanted you to know that I never thought what we did was a mistake."

He slanted her a smile that squeezed her heart with melancholy. "Me either."

She told herself that her physical responses were nothing more than remnants of the past. But the spreading heat and the shudder from head to toe, as if she'd gotten up too fast, called her a liar. She still wanted him, still wanted the wild rush of passion only he could bring out of her.

They were crossing a forbidden line, one that threatened the foundation of their friendship, and their lives.

She had to resist her vulnerability when it came to Noah. She had too many obligations right now. Her father and the store depended on her. That was her job. It was her blood. She couldn't leave it any more than he could leave his work at Seekers. Besides, there could be no room for feelings now. Especially not for Noah. She still needed him to catch the stalker and…*this*… would get in the way.

"I should get ready to go." She hung on to him as if her legs had no bones. "I need to pick up my dress for the party from the store."

His arms, circling her hips, made no move to release her. "You're still in danger, Faith. The IP address belongs to a cybercafe, and that means that anybody can use their computers. I can't go there and examine their computers, either. I'm not law enforcement. The police are going to have to do that, and that's going to take time."

"How long can it take to find who used that particular computer on a particular date and time?" Really, he'd done all the hard work for them. All they had to do was pick up the creep.

"In theory hours, but—"

She cocked her head. "There you go. A few hours, and it'll all be over."

"There are warrants to obtain. And yours isn't a priority case, Faith."

"I can't stay hidden here until the police get around to catching him. I have obligations. The employees expect me to show up at the holiday party tonight."

"Griffin can take your place as the family representative." Noah rocked her gently in his arms, no doubt trying to cajole her into giving in.

"All I have to do is put in an appearance." A compromise. She could make a compromise. "An hour. That's all. Then we can come back here. All safe and sound."

The window above the single desk in the room without a computer shattered. A rock the size of a cantaloupe barely missed Noah and smashed the flat-screen monitor behind him. Noah shielded her body with his, maneuvered her out of harm's way, then pushed her down beneath the desk. "Stay there."

He raced outside.

Did any police department serve this island? She fumbled a hand across the desktop for a phone and found Noah's cell. When Noah didn't return, she ventured out of her hiding place. What if the stalker had jumped him? What if he needed her?

What if that damned stalker was out there waiting for her to come out?

Her gaze bounced around the room, searching for a weapon. It finally landed on the Japanese sword displayed above the only window in the room. Cold wind lashed at her through the broken glass. Her bare feet carefully avoided the shards littering the desk, and she reached for the sword.

Now armed, she crept out of the computer room, down the hallway's carpet runner and into the marble-tiled entrance. The front door stood wide open, wind belting it back and forth on its hinges with a *whap* when the knob banged into the wall.

Fingers of wind stirred the flaps of a box sitting on the flagstone stair.

Sword at the ready, Faith crouched close to look inside.

The box contained cheap travel souvenirs, the kind Faith had collected when she'd traveled to Europe with her family on a buying trip—a Big Ben bank, a four-inch Eiffel Tower, a Leaning Tower snow globe and a mound of postcards, flip-flapping like the dry mocking laughter of ghouls.

"You could go to the police," the topmost postcard read. "But there's no telling what I would do. Don't push me, Faith, or you'll find out."

Noah approached, winded but unhurt. "Don't touch anything."

"I didn't." Faith rocked back on her heels. "Did you get him?"

"He got away." Frustration oozed from every pore of his steaming body.

With the tip of the sword, she scooted the box toward him. "I'm not safe anywhere."

Chapter Six

The line between King County and Pierce County bisected not only Lovan Island, but the house, making it a jurisdiction nightmare when help was needed. Dealing with the officers from two separate departments took longer than Noah had expected. Then they'd had to hitch a ride back to shore with one of the officers since whoever had thrown the rock through the window had first bashed it against the outboard's engine. The force of the destruction reeked of rage.

At the marina, they found the rental car with locks superglued and all four tires knifed in the sidewalls so they would have to be replaced, garnering them more quality time with the Seattle P.D. No one had seen anything and the security tape had conveniently vanished from the lone camera monitoring the parking lot.

Noah wanted to bundle Faith into his jet and fly her to the other end of the world, away from the stalker who was growing bolder and more violent by the day. But he knew she would never agree.

While Noah called a glazier to replace the window and arranged for someone to pick up and fix Ben's boat, Faith called her office, holding strong to her determination to attend the damned employee holiday party. "Sergio, I hate to bother you when your plate's already full, but I have a huge favor to ask. Do you think you could run my dress to the security desk at my condo?"

She turned to Noah. "What size suit do you wear?"

He told her and she repeated the information to Sergio, thanking him profusely for adding a suit from Byrne's men's line to his drop.

"Sergio's got a good eye," she said, at his silent question, and dropped her phone back into her purse. "And you didn't pack a suit."

On the plus side, their side trip to the police station to give a statement about the attacks garnered them the promise of a warrant request to search the cybercafe's computers. On the minus side, the officer taking their statements had politely refused Noah's offer to run Ben's Bloodhound program. Even with the new developments in Faith's case, there would be no priority tag for the forensics lab to expedite their analysis. And though he hated to pull strings, Noah figured if he had them, he might as well use them. He put a call in to Falconer to grease the wheels of interagency cooperation. He had a feeling he'd need them before this was through.

By the time they arrived at Faith's condo, it was past five.

"I have less than an hour to get ready," she complained, juggling her dress, his suit—which they'd collected from the front desk—and her overnight bag as the elevator doors opened on her floor. "I wanted to be there before the party started to greet everyone."

Noah almost jabbed the down button at the sight of the three knives impaled in the jamb of Faith's front door. She didn't need this.

When the doorknob to Max Hessel's condo jiggled, Noah scooted Faith behind him. He'd have to check Hessel's where-abouts last night with the P.I. he'd put on Hessel's tail.

All slick and smooth, Hessel blinked at their presence, then whistled at the sight of the knives. "Who'd you piss off, babe?"

"I wish I knew," Faith said on a long breath. "Did you hear anything out of the ordinary last night? Today?"

Hessel's brown eyes were a tad bloodshot and the back of one hand showed knuckles that looked as if they'd gone through a cheese grater. "Sorry, babe, but you know how well these walls are soundproofed. A bomb could go off and no one would hear it."

Neighborhood watch was alive and strong, Noah thought, sarcasm oozing. *And call her "babe" one more time, jerk, and you'll have a black eye to go with your bruised hand.* "What time did you come in last night?"

Hessel shrugged as if the effort to think past the haze of alcohol was too much. "I don't know. Three. Four, maybe. The knives weren't in the door then."

As if he was likely to notice. "Did you go out today?"

"I've been catching up on business at home."

On a Sunday? Seemed rather ambitious for a guy who'd traipsed home drunk in the wee hours of the morning. Noah nodded at Hessel's scraped knuckles. "What happened to your hand?"

"Oh, that." Hessel tugged on the sleeve of his tan overcoat, spiriting the cuts out of sight. "Close encounter with a parking barrier." He smiled sheepishly. "The barrier won."

Hessel turned to Faith. "You gonna call the cops?"

"Already done."

Hessel started to nod, then seemed to think better of it. "Good. I'd hate for a sweet thing like you to get hurt."

"Where are you going to be if the cops need to talk to you?" Noah asked.

"At the Flying Fish for drinks and dinner with a pretty lady." The lift of lips was no doubt meant to look rakish, but it came across as predatory. "I'm sure talking to the cops can wait till morning. No harm, no foul, right?"

Noah scowled. *Yeah, thanks for your concern, buddy.*

Hessel left.

Faith stared at her front door, key in hand,

but made no move toward it. "Do you think he got in again?"

"If he did, those knifes would be inside." Probably hilt-deep in her mattress.

Noah cleared the apartment, but found no other trace of trespassing. The stalker must have been frustrated by the new locks.

"I'm going to take a shower while we wait for an officer to show up." Faith didn't wait for either permission or acknowledgment, but disappeared into her bedroom. Noah turned on the television and caught up on news, hoping the distraction would allow his brain to make sense out of all the disparate clues the stalker was leaving.

He put a call through to the P.I. following Hessel, but got voice mail and was forced to leave a message.

He flicked through channels, not really seeing anything. Damn stubborn woman. Just like her father. Couldn't see reason, even when it put her life in danger.

Don't care. Flick. *Don't care.* Flick. *Don't care.* Flick, flick, flick.

He tossed the remote onto the coffee table. He might as well try not to breathe as to not care about Faith.

The security desk rang up the police's arrival. Noah answered the knock on the door. As the cop entered, Faith came out of her bedroom bundled in a thick robe, her hair freshly blow-dried, looking much too small and vulnerable. She answered the officer's questions with a wooden quality that worried Noah.

"You don't have to go to this party," Noah said once the officer left.

"I do." Her chin slowly found its way to the familiar stubborn angle. There was no point arguing with her. They both retreated to their rooms to finish getting ready for the party.

Faith was at her desk, checking telephone messages when he reappeared. "My, my, don't you clean up good."

He tugged on one jacket sleeve. "Was there ever a doubt?"

"You forget that the last time I saw you, you were in your hiking boots and khaki shorts phase."

He made a face. "Yeah, what a catch! All skin and bones."

She blushed a deep crimson, highlighting the sweet spray of freckles across her nose.

"Not so skinny. All hard muscle." Her lips quirked to teasing. "So sexy with those big dimples."

He shamelessly flashed those dimples at her. "Yeah?"

"Really."

He wished he'd known that back then. He'd always wondered if their lovemaking had been as good for her as it had been for him. She stood and his gaze skimmed the length of her red power dress, showing curves in all the right places. "You don't look so bad yourself, Ms. Executive."

Her head tilted, and she rewarded him with a smile that spun sunbeams in her eyes. "Thank you, kind sir."

He offered her an elbow. If he couldn't change her mind, then he'd be there to keep her safe. He'd had enough practice at these affairs to know how to circulate.

If nothing else, the party would allow him to chat up some of his most likely suspects.

THEY ARRIVED AT BYRNE'S over an hour late, and though Faith had insisted she needed to be there, she wished it could have been even later. She paused when the elevator doors opened and drew in a long breath as the air exploded with a cacophony of conversations and the ear-thumping pump of Christmas music. Garlands of snowflakes hung from the ceiling and silver tinsel, festooning the café's potted palm trees and ferns, twinkled in the fairy lights around them. The cloying smell of sugar from the chocolate fountain and all the pastries laid out over the tables stirred nausea. As much as she'd insisted on coming to this affair, it was the last place she wanted to be.

But her father expected her to keep up the appearance that everything was perfect, and God forbid she should let grave illness or the threat of an unbalanced stalker get in the way of that "proper" image.

Silently Noah took her coat and checked it in at the temporary coat check Sergio had set up.

She splayed a hand over the bodice of the dress that was suddenly too tight. Give her a business meeting where the objective was defined and her expertise in play, and she could shine. But social affairs where a conversation could take more curves than a mountain road... She shuddered.

She was supposed to be a pro at socializing. Polished manners were supposed to ooze from her pores as naturally as air. After all, she was born to this, had lived and breathed it from day one. But the truth was that large, crowded rooms mainlined queasiness into her veins. Small talk seemed so, well, small, and such a waste of perfectly usable time she could spend to more profitable ends.

What if the stalker was here? What if as Noah suspected, he was one of her own employees? Would she see his evil intent in his eyes?

As she stepped into the café, the butterflies fluttering around her stomach morphed into a swarm of killer bees. Sweaty palms, revving heartbeat, ten-story-stair-climbing breath didn't help the whole picture-perfect posture her father expected her to present at all times.

Easy for him to ask, he wasn't being stalked. Oh, who was she kidding? Even if her father were being stalked, he'd show no feelings. Sometimes she wasn't sure he had any to show, at all.

Noah turned her so she faced him straight on, took one of her hands in both of his, kissed it, and said, "Faith, you are the most ravishing woman here tonight."

It was corny, sure, but his star-shine eyes and his smooth jazz voice made her believe it. Her stiff spine loosened and her body lightened, and as Noah chatted his way across the room to the bar, the usual trek through the combat zone became a comfortable stroll. By the time he ordered a glass of pinot grigio for her, she didn't need the wine to relax.

"You're good at this." She studied him with new admiration. "I thought you hated shindigs like these."

"It's not my favorite way to spend an evening."

"But you look like you're enjoying yourself."

"I learned before elementary school that if Mom or Dad decided I had to attend one of their affairs, I'd have to, and no amount of bitching and moaning was going to change their minds. So I might as well have fun." He shrugged. "I look at it as making music."

She frowned. "You're kidding."

"Nope. A conversation is like a jam session. I take in their looks and mood, and I try to match it. If they're down, I slowly move them up the scale, and see if I can get a smile out of them." He gave her an aw-shucks grin, but she didn't miss his careful study of the crowd. "And you know me. I like to see people smile."

"You are the biggest cornball I know." She pecked a kiss on his cheek and wished for something more. If that rock hadn't shattered the moment this morning, would their common sense have slipped back into passion before she'd climbed down from his lap?

And of course, thoughts of that rock and who had thrown it revved her anxiety all over again, overriding even desire.

Noah's snapping of mental pictures of the crowd didn't help, either. The reason he'd so easily given in to her request to attend the party was no doubt to question possible stalker candidates among her staff. "Who are you looking for?"

One side of his mouth kicked up. "What can I say? People like to talk to me."

"You didn't answer my question."

"Hardeman, Jaworski, Gadwah and New-some for a start."

"Newsome? From Menswear?"

He arched an eyebrow. "Don't tell me you haven't noticed the way he looks at you."

She stammered. "I-I didn't. H-he doesn't. He's married, for goodness sake."

"That doesn't stop some people."

The thought of her ex, Heath, and the way she'd found him pretzeled with that cruise ship chorus girl whammed her between the eyes. He hadn't even had the decency to take his cheating to the woman's cabin. The thought that Newsome, who had a wife and two kids at home, could be stalking her made her queasy all over again. "I guess you're right."

Sergio snaked his way through the crowd, approaching them with an appreciative glance at the length of their outfits and a pleased-punch smile. "Ah, Miss Faith, Mr. Noah, you look like a couple from the pages of *Vogue*."

Noah turned toward Sergio and rewarded him with a warm smile, giving him his undivided attention. "Good choice of suit." He tugged on the charcoal-gray lapels of Byrne's own private label. "You have a good eye for fashion."

"I do." Sergio beamed. "And once I finish my courses, I would like to find a position as a buyer." He turned to Faith with a hopeful look.

"I've already told you that when you're ready, I'd love nothing more than to see you join Byrne's buying team." Her gaze took a circuit of the room, expecting the stalker to jump out at her somehow. But wasn't his ability to be one of the crowd his advantage? He could be any one of these smiling people. "How's everything going?"

"So far, so good," Sergio assured her. "They're all clamoring for your holiday wishes."

Great. "Give me half an hour to circulate, then signal the deejay to take a break."

Sergio pointed at the massive watch gracing his skinny wrist. "Like clockwork." With a nod to Noah, Sergio disappeared once more into the crowd.

Noah squeezed her elbow for encouragement. "Ready?"

She took a deep breath, pasted a smile on her face and nodded. "As I'll ever be."

Noah greeted each sales associate she introduced as if they were an old friend that life had unfairly kept from him, with easy hellos and how-do-you-dos and I'm-so-pleased-to-meet-yous. His hand reached out to shake hands. And his eyes, those secret weapons of disarmament, turned soft and wide, bringing her an unexpected twinge of jealousy at his public ease.

The floor became charged with good feelings. The air around him practically sparkled. Watching him, she could see how tense she'd become in the last month, how the stress had further distanced her from her employees who already saw her as an ice queen.

Still, in none of those faces, none of those handshakes, none of those smiles, could she find a hint that someone wanted her harmed.

"Oh, wow, that's really interesting," a woman she recognized as Susan Lim, the pastry chef, told Noah. And Faith realized she'd zoned out and missed the conversation's flow. "What do you do?"

"I help people find any information they need with my computer," Noah said.

Susan's laugh lilted with a flirtatious tone. "How about a new source for Meyer lemons? I can't find any to save my cheesecake these days."

"Cheesecake?"

"I'm the pastry chef at Byrne's café."

Noah seamlessly dragged Faith back into

the conversation. "Faith, Susan was just telling me about her gift for baking. You remember, we saw on the news that she was participating in the Sweet Sweep of Seattle. I hadn't made the connection of the name until now. Susan, Faith's been bragging about the lemon cheesecake you make for Byrne's."

Faith took Noah's cues. "Congratulations on making the finals! That cheesecake is truly a sin." With Noah there, supporting her, it was easy to slip into the role her grandmother and Rhea, Griffin's mother, had modeled so often for her without falling on her awkwardness. Faith leaned in toward Susan as if to impart a secret. "Don't tell anyone, but I could eat a whole cake all by myself. You're a shoo-in to win. What do you do to get that tartness just right?"

"It's all in the lemons." Susan looked as if she'd already won the grand prize.

They left Susan retelling her cheesecake story to another employee and maneuvered to the next cluster of employees. "Jaworski's sitting by himself at the bar," Noah said into her ear, sending a shiver that warmed the silk back of her dress.

"Okay." She braced herself. "Let's go."

"I have a better chance of getting him to open up to me if you're not within earshot."

"I see." The thought that one of the employees she'd worked so hard to keep happy could want to say something he wouldn't want her to hear sat heavy in her stomach.

"Are you going to be okay by yourself?"

"Of course." She bristled. "I don't need a babysitter. I've been doing this for years."

But as Noah walked away, vertebra by vertebra, her spine cranked with tension that left her feeling like a fish in an ocean of sharks.

NOAH SIDLED UP TO Jaworski sitting at the bar, already deep in his beer. The suit he wore fit him awkwardly, too loose in the shirt, too tight in the pants. His gut spilled over the belt and his reindeer-studded tie hung too low. Resentment traced heavy lines on his well-padded face.

"Hey," Noah said, after he'd ordered a beer and took a seat next to Jaworski. He had to shout a bit to be heard over the music. "Thanks for all your help in understanding how the new merchandise control program connects to the rest of the computer network."

"No problem." Jaworski snorted, then kicked back what was left of his beer. "I hate all that technology, you know."

"I hear you. It takes the humanity out of business."

"You're not kidding. Makes me feel like a frigging robot."

"You've got to remember that machines are stupid, and you'll get along fine."

Jaworski laughed, unconvinced. "Easy for you to say." He spun his beer mug on its base, and his gaze fell on Faith, who was listening attentively to Keith Caldarella, who managed jewelry and accessories.

"So you like the lady boss?" Noah asked casually. From the corner of his eye, he noticed Griffin eyeing him as if he were a nuclear threat. He held hands with his blond paper-doll fiancée, who was dressed in an electric-blue number.

"I hate to say anything, 'cuz she's the boss's kid, you know. But it'd be better if she'd let Hardeman run the show."

"Why's that?"

Jaworski signaled for a refill. "Don't get me wrong. She's good at some things, but she's too soft, you know, and the guys yank her chain. Mr. H wouldn't take the crap she does. Know what I mean?"

Noah shrugged. "It's a family business. Family takes over."

"Yeah, some of us have to bust our butts to get anywhere, and in walks this ice princess, and she gets the big prize. Nepotism." He shook his head. "Doesn't seem fair."

"Doesn't look good for the old man." Noah let his implication hang.

Jaworski rubbed his chin, pouting out his lower lip as if the beer had gone flat and bitter. "Guess it's time to start looking for another job."

"Because you couldn't work for a woman?"

Jaworski looked at him as if he were dense. "'Cuz if the old man croaks, ain't no way she can stop the store from collapsing. Not with Federated already positioned with its two new stores to slide Byrne's right off its weak hold."

Did Faith realize business was so bad? Or was Jaworski exaggerating? Maybe Noah had been looking in the wrong place all along. What if the threat to Faith was coming from an outside competitor? Something to research.

"Hey, Johnny!" Two of Jaworski's laughing pals pulled him off his stool and dragged him to the dance floor where girls much too young for them waited.

Noah studied the room, looking for his next target, when he caught a flash of bright blue. Tugging his fiancée along, Griffin was glad-handing his way toward Faith.

The slide of Noah's gaze connected with Faith's across the room, and the jolt he'd felt twelve years ago, the first time she'd looked at him, bolted through him. Her smile widened, spreading sunshine that warmed him. And he had to remind himself how bad the burn had hurt. Trouble was, he realized, he wanted her now even more than then, and that wasn't good.

He turned his back on her and aimed himself at Hardeman.

Hardeman, Philip Byrne's right-hand man, was tall and thin. Steel-colored hair, cropped old-school business—short, covered his scalp. Bags, years in the growing, pooched below his eyes. Gravity had not been kind to his jowls. He sat at a table in the middle of the fray, a king at court.

Taking advantage of a lull, Noah joined him, shot the breeze for a few minutes before easing into questions. "Do you think Faith can handle management of something as complicated as Byrne's?"

Hardeman shot him an appraising look. "Faith can handle anything. She has her mother's grace, her grandmother's vision and her father's determination."

"But?"

Hardeman bobbled his head from side to side, acknowledging imperfection. "She's missing a bit of seasoning."

"So you'd feel okay, if for some reason her father didn't recover, and you had to take orders from Faith?"

"I'm there to help her with whatever she needs."

Which didn't sound like a bitter man, waiting for the ingenue to fail so he could take over what he felt was his due. On the other hand, someone with takeover plans wouldn't announce them, especially to him.

"Listen, I'm an old man, but I'm no fool. I know something's going on and that it probably has nothing to do with the computer system's security you're checking out. I'm guessing blackmail."

Hardeman cocked an eye at Noah, searching for an answer. Noah shrugged. "I hear Federated is making things tough."

Hardeman waved Noah's comment away. "Federated wants our assets, sure, but Faith's scratched out a nice market slice for Byrne's. We're not in any danger of losing it unless she decides she wants to sell."

"You think maybe there's someone else out there who'd want to blackmail her?"

"Wouldn't be the first time." Hardeman assessed Noah with a shrewd eye. "But it's not coming from me. Five more years, and I'm heading south. Arizona. New Mexico. Some place warm where my arthritic bones won't complain all the time. I knew coming in that I'd never reach the top spot. I stayed because Philip's a friend, and he's given me free rein to maximize my talents."

Hardeman nodded toward Faith, laughing with a gaggle of young associates. "I've known Faith since the day she was born. Saw her go through a hard time after her grandmother passed on. She shouldn't have jumped into marriage with that Jamieson fellow. He was all wrong for her, even if Philip thought otherwise. If she needs help, she can trust me with her life."

"Oh, hey!" Hardeman lifted a hand as he spotted someone in the crowd. "I've been trying to corner Ernest Sayers all evening. You'll have to excuse me." He rose, extending a hand. "It's good to know Faith has a friend watching over her."

Noah dropped his empty glass on a passing waiter's tray. Faith was with Griffin—paper-doll fiancée nowhere in sight—and though Faith's smile was tacked on in a perfectly civil manner, the too-tight tension of it made him think she wasn't liking Griffin's big-brother words of wisdom. She didn't quite look as if she needed rescuing yet, so Noah latched on to his next victim.

Kit Gadwah trolled the food table like a tiger angling for prey. After each selection, he scowled at the festivities. Noah especially didn't like the way he was following Faith's path across the room.

Noah grabbed a plate and started down the line, feigning great interest in the spread of pastries and mounds of strawberries, chunks of pineapple and squares of pound cake waiting to be dipped into the chocolate fountain. "What do you recommend?"

"It is all delicious." The lilt of Gadwah's

voice was nearly lost in the ceaseless pump of music. "The pastry chef here has excellent taste."

They talked shop until Gadwah's demeanor thawed a few degrees. But before Noah could grill him, the music stopped and Faith accepted a microphone from her assistant. "I want to thank you all for coming tonight. Byrne's couldn't operate without its employees, and I look forward to this day every year when I can remind each and every one of you personally how much we appreciate the hard work you do—"

"She says pretty things," Gadwah said, teeth all but bared, "but she does not mean them. I was supposed to have total control over the system. That was my only condition when I accepted the job. There is one tiny glitch, and she calls in an outside source."

"She was trying to lighten your load since you were busy with the inventory tracking system."

Gadwah's midnight eyes narrowed to slits. His jaw worked in a tight circle. "I have everything under control. I do not need you to tell me how to keep my systems safe."

Anger oozed out of Kit, as noxious as

mustard gas. The kind of deep-seated anger that could have smashed an outboard engine to bits.

Noah watched the IT manager stride to the elevator and grind the button. The man had a grudge, and the kind of knowledge that could have bypassed Ben's security system. He might not have been able to get inside the house, but he'd gotten close enough to terrorize Faith.

As FAITH LEFT the group of teenage associates from the juniors department, Griffin cornered her. Tara, his fiancée, glared at them from the bar. "Where have you been?"

"You heard about the sketchy people coming to the office?" she asked, not really wanting to deal with her big brother's protectiveness right now. "I just had to get away until the police could deal with them."

"You can't just disappear like that without saying anything. I was worried sick. I didn't know if one of those men had gotten to you."

In the frantic storm of his gray eyes she saw that he had truly worried about her welfare. "I'm sorry. I should have realized that you'd be worried."

"Ever since that guy arrived—" he jerked his chin in Noah's direction "—you've been acting weird. Not trusting me. What's he saying about me that's put you off?"

"Nothing." The secret she'd agreed to keep from Griffin weighed on her. She had no reason to keep the stalker information from him, but she couldn't bring herself to tell him she was in over her head. He'd take it as a sign of weakness, and right now, she couldn't afford to let him know he was one up on her. "A friend of Noah's has a place close by, and we thought it would be good to get away while the police dealt with the chat-room weirdos."

"You should have come to me. I would have helped you."

"You're right. I should have let you know what was going on."

The storm in Griffin's eyes calmed and his voice softened. "I've had our lawyer contact the site owner and slap them with a cease and desist order. Last time I checked, the false information about you was wiped. If it comes up again, Norcross has got orders to hit them with a suit."

"Thank you, Griffin. It's good to know you're there for me."

"Can I get you anything? You look a little pale."

She shook her head and attempted a smile. "I think I've reached my limit for tonight."

He reached to take her arm. "I'll take you home."

"What about Tara?"

"She won't mind."

Faith deftly maneuvered out of his hold. "That's okay. You keep circulating. I'll have Noah take me home."

Griffin's jaw worked as if he were chewing words. "I need to talk to you tomorrow about the budget numbers for some of your projects. You're going to need to cut."

"Talk to Sergio and have him make room on my agenda for a meeting."

With a curt nod, Griffin was off, and Faith let out a long sigh.

Crowds sucked her energy like a horde of vampires. She wanted to sink into a bath of bubbles all the way up to her chin and stay there until her skin pruned. *Half an hour more, and you can go home.*

Sergio sneaked up behind her and tapped her on the shoulder. "It's time, *mija.*"

With a gulp of air and a shoring up of her

spine, she accepted the microphone from her assistant. She hadn't had time to prepare a speech and had no idea what she was going to say. Her gaze skimmed the crowd, but it wasn't until it landed on Noah, looking at her as if she shone as brightly as the sun that words spilled out and her genuine appreciation for her employees flowed.

To the roar of applause, she handed the microphone back to the deejay. As she started to look for Noah, Sergio approached her with a package wrapped in red foil and silver ribbons. "This came for you."

"Who is it from?"

Sergio shook his dark head, tumbling curls over his forehead. "Security handed it to me to give to you." He pointed at the card. "It says Happy Holidays. Should I put it with the others?"

"Yes, that would be great. I'll deal with it in the morning. Are the parting gifts for the employees ready?"

"Everything is set by the coat-check table." A smug look compressed his face. "They will be so pleased."

Package in tow, Sergio headed for her office, and Faith turned to resume her search for Noah, only to find him at her elbow. "Did you talk to everyone you needed to?"

He nodded. "Ready to blow this Popsicle stand?" Noah asked in a joking tone, no doubt reading the desperation she'd hoped she was masking.

Her breath washed out in relief. "My duty is done. Take me home. *Please.*"

"Your wish is my command." Low laughter rumbled in his chest, taking the edge off her tension. "Let me get your coat."

Having retrieved her velvet wrap from the coat check, he helped her into it. "You handled the evening like a pro."

"It's what's expected." By the employees. By her father. By her grandmother. The weight of those expectations nearly crushed her chest. "Think Hardeman will give me a favorable critique when he reports to Daddy?"

"An A-plus at the very least."

It was her turn to laugh. "Do you have to go back to New Hampshire, Noah? Having you around is good for my ego."

Just as they stepped to the elevator's waiting car, an explosion rocked the building.

Chapter Seven

"Sergio!" Faith's feet didn't wait for her brain to engage. She ran for the stairs and took them two by two up to her office, fear flying behind her, too fresh to quite catch up. Noah matched her pace, his voice echoing in the stairwell as he barked orders into his phone.

In spite of the sprinklers, air thick with smoke greeted them. The papers on her desk crinkled with flames. And Sergio lay crumpled beside the chrome-and-glass desk, the gray carpet soaking up his blood. His face was black. Burns? Debris from the package?

Noah yanked the fire extinguisher off the wall in the hallway and attacked what remained of the burning mess on her desk with a spray of foam.

Panic running a marathon through her veins, Faith dropped to her knees, water staining her red dress, hands hovering above Sergio, not knowing what to do. What had the instructor said in the first-aid course she'd taken years ago? ABC? She couldn't remember what the acronym stood for. B for breathing. Was he breathing? His chest was lying much too still. Her fingers pressed against his jugular, searching for a pulse. "Sergio?"

He moaned.

He was alive. Afraid to move him, she took his hand and held it tightly. "Hang in there. Help is on the way."

This bomb had been meant for her. Now Sergio was hurt. Oh, God, possibly dying because she'd insisted on keeping up appearances at the holiday party. Going after her was one thing; hurting those who depended on her was another. She set her jaw until her teeth hurt. "He's not going to get away with this. I promise."

Outside, sirens shrieked and wailed, coming closer and closer. Sergio's shallow breaths turned to gurgling, and she squeezed his hand harder, willing him to live. "Hang on, Sergio."

Soon the place swarmed with shouts and trampling feet from firemen, paramedics and police.

"You have to let go, Faith," a voice penetrated the crazed hum of the room to reach her frazzled brain. She looked up at Noah, his warm hands trying to pry her cold, bloodstreaked fingers from Sergio's. "The paramedics are here to help."

"You take care of him," she ordered the paramedics as she released Sergio's hand. "He's to get the best of everything."

"Yes, ma'am, they all do." The paramedic prodded and pricked, hooking Sergio up to portable machines and an IV drip.

"You tell the staff at the hospital."

"Yes, ma'am." She could tell the agreement was his tool of choice to get rid of a crazy woman.

Not that it mattered. The important thing was to get Sergio medical care as soon as possible. She'd call the hospital and ensure that all his needs were met. He would get the best. He would survive. He had to.

She allowed Noah to help her up and support her shaking body. The paramedics hefted Sergio onto a gurney and rolled him out.

When she'd phoned Noah for his help, she'd been scared at the intrusion into her home, but not once had she thought her stalker would go this far—that he would hurt others to get to her. She'd thought she could handle this nuisance alone and, with Noah's help, that she could keep her personal inconvenience a secret.

She had to make things right. For Sergio. For everyone who worked for her.

Blinking back tears, she pushed off Noah and headed for the officer in charge. She needed to stay cool and calm. Screaming and tears could come later.

In a sea of uniforms, the detective was the only one wearing a suit—a cheap, brown, off-the-rack two-piece that looked slept in—and even she couldn't mistake him for anything other than a cop. There was an us-versus-them coldness in his hooded eyes as he viewed the scene, an alertness to his stance that said any sudden move could result in his weapon going from holster to hand in a flash. But that threat didn't scare her. She might be a foot shorter and ninety pounds lighter, but she had no intention of losing this standoff. Sergio was hurt, possibly dying. She couldn't let that crime go unsolved.

"That bomb was meant for me." Faith uttered every word precisely, with perfect control, although everything in her shook with rage. Her father would be proud. "This man is my assistant. He's an innocent bystander. If he dies because of this bomb, I will hold your department personally responsible."

The detective blinked, the mismatch of her fragile looks and the authoritative tone hitting two separate parts of his brain, scrambling it. He stuck a well-chewed toothpick in his mouth. "Ma'am?"

"Your officers have told me on at least two separate occasions that they couldn't do anything about the stalker making my life hell until someone got hurt. Well, someone got hurt. What are you going to do about finding the man who did this?"

"We'll do our best." His face a mask of poached displeasure, the detective started to turn away.

Faith held on to his elbow with clawed fingers, earning her a warning scowl, but she didn't let go. "Your best isn't good enough. This man is a human being, not another case on your docket. His name is Sergio Sandoz. He's been working at Byrne's for five years to support a younger brother and sister—" oh, God, someone would have to tell them "—and going to school at night to earn a degree in fashion merchandising. Not once has he complained about the burden. He comes in every day with a smile on his face." All that seemed a pitiful way to sum up a man's life. "He didn't deserve to have a bomb meant for me explode in his face. Do you understand?"

"Yes, ma'am, and I'll appreciate your cooperation with our investigation."

Detecting a note of sympathy in his eyes, she relented her forceful stand. Time was of the essence, so she laid out the situation. "I have no idea who this stalker is, although I suspect that it's someone who works for Byrne's. You can catch up by reading the previous reports I've made to your associates. I don't know where the package came from. The typed note simply said Happy Holidays. I didn't think anything of it, because several employees brought gifts. The security guards were under orders to inspect badges."

Then she thought of Max Hessel and Noah's suspicions about him. "You might want to question them to see if someone other than a guest dropped off the package." She pointed at Noah, standing beside her. "Mr. Kingsley is a security expert, and he's been trying to help me unmask the stalker without arousing suspicions from my staff. He's gone over our computer systems."

Noah gave the detective a quick overview of his findings. "You might want to add Kit Gadwah to your list of people to talk to."

"Kit?" Faith asked.

"He's one angry man."

Faith swallowed hard. The nightmare was only getting worse.

The detective's right eyebrow arched as he scribbled a note, his hand motion matching the jitterbug of his toothpick. "I'll need printouts and a copy of your private detective's report."

Noah nodded. "As soon as it's safe to go back to Ms. Byrne's condo."

"I'll get you a safety detail. Right now I need you and Ms. Byrne to clear the room so my team can record the evidence." His gaze cranked over to Faith. "Keep your employees calm and contained. Officers will want to interview every guest before they leave. That includes you."

"Of course. I'll make sure you have full cooperation."

Noah put a protective hand on her elbow and held her in place. "We'll get the interview done quickly, then I'm taking you to a safe place."

She shook her head, determined. "I'm staying. These are my employees. I'm responsible for each and every one of them."

"Let someone else handle—"

"This is *my* family's store, not some chain with a faceless CEO. The employees expect to hear from *me*."

"Your stalker's turned on you, Faith."

He swiveled her toward the soggy burned mess that was her desk, the stain of Sergio's blood still fresh on the gray carpet. All that could go wrong streaked through her brain, all the things over which she had no control, all the ways she'd tried so hard to keep the situation together and still managed to fail. "I haven't done anything to encourage him."

"You don't need to." Noah's voice was soft and low, but an undercurrent of warning stirred beneath. "His perceptions are skewed. He sees you as his possession."

Noah's usually calm-sea eyes flared with

cold heat. "He ordered you to get rid of me," Noah said, "and you didn't obey. Now he's punishing you."

She got what Noah was saying, but her father would expect her to be strong, to put up a solid front for the employees. It was the proper thing to do. "I need to stay. Sergio was badly hurt." She willed Noah to understand. "He might not survive."

"That bomb could have killed you. Your safety comes first."

She shook her head. "No, my secret could very well have cost Sergio his life. I owe it to my employees to let them know the risk they're taking by simply showing up to do their jobs."

She swallowed hard, realizing she would have to tell her staff about the stalker. Her father would be furious at her showing weakness in such a public forum, but she had to protect them as well as herself. "Stay here and get as much information as you can from the officers about the bomb and who might have sent it. I'm going downstairs to talk the my employees."

"I'm not letting you out of my sight."

"I'll be fine. The stalker's not going to strike again. Not with all these cops here."

She made a move to walk past Noah, but his hand flashed out and blocked her path. Legs apart, free arm slightly bent, he looked like a gunslinger squaring off. "You go nowhere alone until your stalker is caught."

Annoyed now when there was so much to do, she tried to plow past him, but he held fast and they ended up doing a slow revolving dance. His face was set. There was no give. She wasn't going to win this bout. And truth was, she would feel safer with Noah watching her back.

"Let's go, then." She strode toward the door. Noah stayed glued to her side. Though everything inside her screamed, and her failures trotted behind her like a pack of wild dogs, she forced herself to remain outwardly calm.

Halfway down the stairs, they ran into Griffin.

His eyes widened at the sight of her, then narrowed at the sight of Noah. "Faith, thank God. You're okay. What happened?"

"Someone sent a bomb wrapped in a package and…" a hand went to her heart "…it exploded in Sergio's face."

"Is he all right?"

Too rattled to stand still, she started back down the stairs, with Griffin on one side and Noah on the other. Presidents should have this much determined muscle protecting them. "I don't know. They took him away by ambulance."

"What do you need me to do?" Griffin asked.

No questions. No arguments. At that moment, she could have kissed him for understanding that the employees came first. "The police want to talk to everyone before they leave. The officers need a place to set up."

"I've got it covered. Go home."

She shook her head. "Later. I need to let everyone know what's going on."

As all three pushed through the café's doors, Tara, Griffin's fiancée, rushed toward Griffin in a blur of electric-blue silk, her face full of fear. She grabbed his hands and hung on to them. "Where have you been?" Then her gaze, just as charged as her dress, landed on Faith, and her delicate nose twitched as she caught the scent of smoke on Faith's clothes. "I want you to take me home, Griff. Right now."

"Not now, Tara." Steel chilled his voice,

iced his eyes. "In case you hadn't noticed, we're in the middle of a crisis here."

"That's *her* problem, not yours. Take me home." The razor tone of her voice neatly chiseled her upset at Griffin's misplaced loyalty. Not that Faith gave a hoot. She had a much larger problem to deal with right now than Tara's self-centered snit. She bumped Noah on the arm and pointed toward the now-quiet deejay's stand, signaling her intention.

"It's my problem, too." Griffin took Tara by the shoulders and sat her down forcefully into a chair. "Wait here. I'll have the cops talk to you first, then you can take a cab home."

Griffin headed toward the two officers trying to contain the frightened crowd.

Because she didn't want to look like some princess in need of a babysitter, Faith took Noah's hand as if he were her date, and strode toward the deejay who handed her the microphone she'd asked for.

"Could I have everyone's attention, please?" She waited while the crowd turned toward her. Noah's palm, warm and wide on the small of her back, calmed the wild bees swarming in her gut.

"Byrne's will be closed tomorrow so that the police may conduct their investigation," she said. "The media will be alerted and a formal announcement made at a press conference tomorrow morning."

Running the Christmas season without full staffing would be tough, but when her employees came to work, they deserved to know that they would not die on the job. They weren't in the military; they were working at a department store. Forgetting all about the image of strength she was supposed to be modeling, she told them about the stalker, and her fears.

"Although I would like all of you to continue working through our busy holiday season, I won't hold it against you if you feel you need to stay away from the store for safety's sake until the stalker is caught. I will hold your job open for you, and welcome you back once this crisis is over."

She pointed toward the makeshift interview tables set up by the elevators. "The officers will need to talk to each of you before you can leave. Given the circumstances, you will be paid for your time. I would appreciate your full cooperation with the officers' questions."

She handed the microphone back to the

deejay, asked him to play a background of soothing music, then did what she was trained to do—circulate, calm and listen. Her heart swelled as employee after employee assured her they would come back to work as soon as the store reopened.

Though Noah remained seemingly relaxed at her side, she noted his careful study of every person and every movement in the room, his hand on her hip ready to draw her away at the slightest hint of danger. Faith asked each employee she talked to about the package, but no one seemed to have noticed who'd brought it.

Hours later, after the police let the last of her employees go, she suddenly felt lost. The adrenaline she'd run on for the last few hours was wearing off. Her head pounded from the strain of the performance. Her best one so far, and her father had missed it. Would he even have noticed? Or would it have fallen under the "expected behavior" column? Catch them doing good had never been her father's policy.

She didn't care. The time had come at last to accept that she would never please her father. As long as she knew she'd performed well, that's all that counted.

As long as she'd had something to do, she'd held herself together, but now she was on the edge of falling apart. A silent quake of tears rumbled in her chest, but she could not let them fall. There was still too much to do tonight before she could let the flood flow into the absorbing feathers of her pillow.

Could you hold me? her eyes begged Noah at his silent question.

He took her into his arms, softening the hard edge of her fears. "You're shaking."

"I'll be okay." She closed her eyes and drank him in. "I need to make a stop at the hospital and check on Sergio." Make sure he had the care he needed. "His brother and sister." She swallowed hard. "How am I going to tell them their brother's accident is my fault?"

"It's not your fault. You didn't send that package."

"I sent Sergio up to my office with it."

"You couldn't know what was inside."

All logical answers, but none that would soothe her conscience.

Noah kissed the top of her head tenderly. "We can't stay at your condo tonight."

"The police are sending extra patrols."

"Fat lot of good that does us twenty-two stories up. I had my sister, Joanna, book us a suite at the King's Arms."

One of the hotels in the chain owned by his family. "A hotel won't be as secure as my condo. Anybody can walk in."

"There'll be a pack of reporters waiting for you at your place. Nobody will know where we are at the hotel. Joanna arranged for a suite in my mother's maiden name."

Nobody had known about the island, either, and her stalker had found them there. She was beginning to think he had some sort of supernatural power. But she'd run out of fight for tonight. With a nod, she agreed to Noah's plan. "We'll need a change of clothes for tomorrow. I'll grab some things from the store before we go."

At least the police were taking the threats to her safety seriously now, making good on the search warrant for the cybercafe and the sex-fantasy chat room, ordering extra patrols around her home and the store.

None of that altered the fact that no one knew who the stalker was. And getting a restraining order, for all the good they did, against a ghost was impossible.

Noah shifted from foot to foot standing in the middle of Philip Byrne's hospital room while Faith washed up in the small bathroom off her father's private room. Of course, she couldn't show herself to her unconscious father with a hair out of place or a streak of smoke on her cheek. Never mind that she could have died tonight.

He stepped closer to Philip Byrne's unmoving form. At seventeen, the efficiency of Philip Byrne's payback had scarred Noah. Not that he'd realized that for years.

Funny how the old man didn't look so imposing now under white hospital sheets, attached by a web of tubes to machines keeping tabs on his heart and his pulse. He was older, thinner than Noah remembered. His blond hair had turned white and grown sparse, his skin the color of old paper.

Water ran in the bathroom, a discordant hiss against the beeps of the machinery attached to Philip Byrne. "For twelve years I've wanted to tell you to go to hell."

But kicking a man when he was down wasn't his style.

"Faith's in trouble." For a moment, Noah

couldn't speak through the gush of anger jetting through his bloodstream.

But Faith was the one thing that linked them—her welfare, her happiness. And because of Faith, he could almost forgive Philip Byrne his sins.

"You've taught her well. She's handling the situation like a trooper." Noah snorted. "She keeps all her feelings trapped tight inside. Just like you. But it's killing her. Is that what you want for your daughter?"

Not a flinch, not a flutter from the body on the bed.

"I'd like to lay the blame for her situation at your feet," Noah continued. "But this time, I do owe you an apology. Her close call tonight is my fault."

He looked away from the unmoving body and focused on the beige fleck on the linoleum. "I shouldn't have moved into her condo. The stalker misread my intentions to protect her. He sees me as competition, and he took his anger out on Faith. And now…" Noah shook his head. "Now, there's no going back. I have to stay or her stalker will hurt her."

Noah didn't really expect a response from Philip Byrne, but his gaze went back to the old man's slack face. "That's right. She's being stalked. By someone who works for you. Or someone in competition with you. Either way, it's someone who knows her well. And he's terrorizing her, putting her life in danger. But she doesn't say a word, because she thinks that's what you expect. And, of course, it is."

The constant onslaught of worries and tension since he'd arrived in Seattle sawed through Noah. Fists tight with nothing to punch, Noah swallowed the rising growl.

"Tonight, that stalker sent her a bomb wrapped as a holiday gift."

Was Noah imagining the faster pulse?

"She's fine," Noah said, not quite understanding why he felt the need to reassure her father. "For now. Her assistant's the one who took the hit for her."

This time, there was no need to question the spike in activity on the machines. An alarm sounded.

"I'm going to take care of Faith," Noah vowed. "Make sure nothing happens to her. I give you my word."

A nurse clipped in to check on the machines, shooting Noah a questioning look.

He shrugged. The nurse adjusted a dial here, another there, and finally left.

He might not have a future in Faith or Philip Byrne's lives, but for Faith's sake, he wanted her to have what she needed. "You should be proud of your daughter, you miserable bastard."

What was the point of this? It wasn't as if the old man could apologize, beg for forgiveness, or do any damn thing to change.

"She's working so hard to win your approval that she's not living her life. She's just going through the motions of what she thinks you want from her. She doesn't deal well with failure. And this particular failure is sapping the sunshine right out of her." Noah's chest constricted, his throat burned. "It's time to let her go."

A thin, thready voice came from Philip Byrne's bed. Noah thought it said, "I am proud of her."

The water cut out in the bathroom, shutting off the screen of static. The handle turned. The light clicked off.

"Then tell her." Given the old man's condition, Noah could not make himself add *before it's too late.*

Chapter Eight

News of the bomb at Byrne's holiday party had spread fast, and a circus of news crews with cameras and light poles and microphones jockeyed for positioning to get a fifteen-second sound bite from Faith when she left the store, and once again at the hospital. She'd given them a statement outside the store and didn't want to go through the exercise again. The jackals could go elsewhere for their piece of pain to feed the public and their ratings.

A wave of gratitude crested through her when Noah, without needing to be asked, hustled her away from the blood-seeking reporters and through a maze of starkly-lit corridors. They ended up at an exit next to Dumpsters and rumbling air ducts, glaring under harsh sodium-vapor lights, but otherwise dark and empty.

Noah scanned the area and jerked his chin toward the sidewalk. "We'll head down a couple of blocks and grab a cab."

They jogged two blocks, with only the staccato sound of her heels on concrete trailing them. Noah flagged a cab and they were on their way to safety.

A security guard waited to meet them at a back entrance of the hotel to take them straight to their suite.

Not until the door of their suite locked behind them did Faith let go of the breath turning sour in her rigid lungs. Without a word, she headed to the bathroom, turned the spigot on hot, shed her clothes and let steam fill the bathroom. As the sweat and soil of the evening gurgled down the drain, silent tears joined the spray of water.

Exhausted from the strain of the day, she wanted nothing more than the oblivion of sleep, but sleep wouldn't come alone in the vast emptiness of the king-size bed draped with cold sheets. Once again, like a compass needle, she found herself seeking Noah.

With his computer out of reach at her condo, Noah had taken every sheet of hotel stationery, covered them with handwriting that might pass for hieroglyphics and spread them over the sitting room's golden carpet. His red tie snaked half on, half off the oval coffee table as if he'd tossed it aside without looking. His stained suit jacket hung haphazardly from the striped arm of the love seat. His shirt was half unbuttoned and his shirtsleeves were rolled up past his elbows, revealing sinewy forearms. His mussed look and intense concentration made for an unexpectedly sexy combination.

Pulled by the powerful draw of his solid body, she stepped into the sitting room. If she asked, those strong arms would close around her, and she would feel warm and safe again. She curled her fingers into her palms, the sweet ache in her belly a pulse she couldn't answer, and headed for the more cautious refuge of a chair. She would not give her all-seeing stalker any more reason to hurt Noah. She already had too much pain on her conscience.

Swaddled in a plush hotel bathrobe, she perched on the edge of a beige armchair, pushed against the wall like the rest of the furniture, and rounded the bare soles of her feet toward each other. "What are you doing?"

He frowned at the grid of papers. "A flow chart of everything we know."

She leaned in closer and marveled at his memory. He'd reconstructed every e-mail, every gift, every contact the stalker had sent and made down to the last detail.

He rocked back on his heels. "Seeing it like this helps me think."

"What are you hoping to find?"

"A pattern. A timeline. A voice. Something that'll click."

"A voice?"

"Ben's been doing some research with linguistics."

"Sorry, you lost me."

"People tend to talk in certain ways, and that pattern shows up in their writing, too. So Ben and his scientists analyzed a slew of documents and found that you can compare known documents with questioned documents and identify the similarities, then apply a statistical analysis and give a degree of certainty to a questioned document. It's still in the testing stage."

"Did you find a word pattern in the stalker's notes?"

Mouth a flat line, he scratched at his

temple. "Something's off." He pointed to the sheets with the blue scribbles. "See how neat and tidy the pattern is. He's leaving you notes and gifts, as if he's wooing you." His hand moved to the sheets with the red scribbles. "But then, there's the chat room setup. The attack at the island. The bomb. Those all happened after I got here. It's like he lost his temper, then cranked himself back under control."

Noah scrubbed a hand through his hair. "I'd give just about anything to feed all this data, along with the cybercafe's hard drives, into Ben's Bloodhound program and see what comes up."

Faith pressed her palms together and anchored them tightly between her knees. She knew the answer didn't lie there. "What we need is to draw him out of hiding."

Noah grunted, and she couldn't tell if it was agreement or dismissal. "He wants me," she said. "Let's use me."

Noah's armor-piercing gaze shot up to meet hers. "No."

One word, said with power and finality, but she couldn't let his dismissal slide. She'd had a lifetime of following rules and look where it had gotten her. Her pulse galloped, but her hands and her feet and her smile never betrayed her fear. "You have a better plan?"

"We'll keep tracking. Sooner or later, he'll make a mistake. They all do. And we'll get him."

Faith couldn't wait that long. Something needed to happen. Soon. Before she lost everything. And because she trusted Noah with her life, she was willing to put herself on the line to end this nightmare. "It's taking too long. It's hurting my employees and my business. It's got to stop."

His penetrating gaze connected with hers, making her shiver. "I'm not letting you dangle yourself as bait."

Guilt made her play an ace she'd had no intention of using. Especially not on Noah. "You're not in charge."

"You asked for my help," Noah reminded her, voice tight.

But Sergio's charred face would not stop haunting her, and she had to lay that ghost to rest. Only the knowledge that her stalker would hurt no one else could achieve that mercy.

"To get the stalker, we'll have to sink to his

level." Her skin prickled. Her breath burned. But she allowed not a crack of her composure to show, not a tell of weakness to manifest.

"I'm not risking you."

Like her father, Noah sought to shield her. She loved him for his passion to protect, but although she'd played the compliant daughter for most of her life, she wasn't weak, and she had to disavow Noah of that notion. Becoming bait was the best way to end her stalker's spree of terror. "He wants me. Only I can give him what he wants. With all your experience and your resources, you could help the police set up a sting. The risk is minimal."

His raised eyebrow said he thought she'd watched one too many bad cop shows. "It's not that simple, Faith. The Seattle police aren't going to welcome a civilian telling them how to run their investigation."

"Suggest, then. You're good at making people think your ideas are theirs."

"Faith—"

"I'd rather do this with you watching my back. I trust you, Noah. Like I trust no one else in this world. But with or without your help, I have to do this. I have to end it. Use me. Before there's another Sergio." *Before you get hurt.*

Silence swelled like a cancer, the malignancy growing, eating away at the fragile bonds of their friendship. If she pressed Noah, she risked losing the friend she loved. But if she didn't, she risked losing the business that had taken her family three generations to build. Without Byrne's what did she have?

Nothing.

His probing gaze suddenly felt as intimate as a caress. "We still have other options."

"But not the luxury of time."

Understanding he needed space to come to the same conclusion, she waited, breath trapped high in her chest. Pressure built until it felt as if she would explode.

He ran the tips of his fingers along her cheek. "Okay. But we do it my way."

Faith nodded, grateful she would not have to face her unseen enemy alone.

FAITH HAD FALLEN ASLEEP curled up on the love seat. Noah wrapped a blanket around her shoulders, tucked it in close, and risked a stolen kiss on her silky cheek. She didn't look so tough with her face scrubbed clean, the sweep of freckles across her nose unmasked. No, she looked too much like the teenage bombshell who'd stolen his heart with a smile.

The twitch of a nightmare pleated her forehead, and cut short the pang of sharp need punching through his gut. He moved away, wracking his brain for a way to keep her safe.

He hated ultimatums.

Faith hadn't thought her plan through. Speed wouldn't get her the release she wanted, but she couldn't see past getting her life back on its routine track.

But he knew better than anyone that, when Faith wanted something, nothing stopped her. If he didn't watch her back, she'd find a way to get herself killed.

What he should do is find a way to cage her. So what if she hated him? At least she'd be alive.

Teeth clenched, he swiveled back to the flow chart on the floor. He had to buy time to run Bloodhound on the café's computers. They were the way to the stalker's identity. In the meantime, there was someone else he could consult that was good with patterns.

He pulled out his cell phone and dialed. Although night was thick outside the drawn curtains of the suite, and his intended party was three time zones away, pushing the clock close to 4:00 a.m. in Massachusetts, he knew the ring would not wake Brynna Reed. He knew that she would answer. She never slept at night. Sometimes he wondered if she slept at all.

When the line connected, he spoke first, getting straight to the point—her preferred modus operandi. "Bryn, it's Noah Kingsley. I have a favor to ask."

Silence met him. He'd debated making the call, knowing his request would stir up a river of emotions. He also knew that Brynna had harnessed those dark emotions toward a greater good. She'd helped a lot of people escape the same dire circumstances she'd barely survived, and he wished she would give herself the same release she gave them. But she was still trapped, unable to quite leave her painful past behind.

"I need your expertise, Brynna."

"I'm just a small-town private eye. Cheating spouses and insurance fraud. I doubt there's anything I can give you that you don't already know how to get."

"A woman's life is at stake. She's being stalked, and she doesn't know by whom. He's getting bolder. Tonight he sent her a bomb disguised as a Christmas present, and now her assistant is clinging to life in a hospital critical-care unit. I need help figuring him out before he hurts anyone else, and from what I saw on your computer last June, you're the go-to expert."

"I have no idea what you're talking about."

Saving lives was what kept Brynna alive. "I wouldn't have called if a life wasn't at stake. I've kept your secret. I'll continue to keep your secret."

The silence was broken only by a sharp, rapid tattoo, like a nail against metal or a pen against a desktop, tapping in time to Brynna's busy, busy mind.

"I helped you save Abbie," he said, aware of Brynna's need to have no debt.

At long last, breath exploded out of her. "Give me what you have."

Noah laid out the facts, then waited patiently for a response. The one thing he'd learned dealing with her last summer was that you couldn't push Brynna Reed. If you did, all sorts of walls went up, and he didn't have time to dismantle them. Not with Faith ready to throw herself at a madman.

"It's not much to go on," Brynna said, and the sharp clicking resumed like the beat of a racing heart.

"I'll take anything that'll narrow down my search."

After another long silence, Brynna rattled off a profile in a voice totally devoid of emotion, as if she were merely a computer having finished its computation of raw data and come up with a summary analysis. "He sounds like an obsessive-compulsive. His house is most likely in immaculate condition. Everything with a place and everything in its place. He doesn't do anything by half measures. He's a collector. Whatever grabs his attention risks becoming an obsession. Whatever makes up his collection, it'll be his most prized possessions. He's going to be particularly possessive about his property. And make no mistake, he considers Faith his property."

Noah scrunched his eyes closed, the thought of Faith as property a weight against his heart. "Why would he keep his identity secret if he's so sure he's in love with her, and her with him?"

"You're asking for specifics, and all I can tell you is my general gut impression from all the cases I've worked."

Sad cases, each and every one. "What? You can't tell me his age, height and address?" he joked, and earned a rare, small burst of laughter from her.

Just as quickly, she turned serious again. "Men like these don't give up. You can throw them in jail, and the minute they're out, they'll go right back to doing what got them arrested."

Another dire statistic he hadn't yet shared with Faith. Still he sensed a deeper hesitation in Brynna. "There's something you're not telling me."

The hard, fast clicking again. "You know I'm not FBI, right? You know I never took official profiling courses, that I flunked out of the police academy?"

For breaking a fellow trainee's nose because he'd made repeated, unwanted advances toward her. Behavior unbecoming of an officer, she'd been told during her debriefing. But Noah would take her gut over any theory-taught profiler. What she'd endured, what she'd seen, gave her an edge nobody wanted to earn. "You have something no book can teach."

Rattled breath vibrated through the line. "The chat-room humiliation and the bomb..."

"What about them?"

"They don't fit with the rest."

His instincts had been right. "Something about them felt off. No threes. Messy hits-and-runs. Not tight, controlled anger like the rest."

"Maybe he's losing control. Becoming frustrated."

The wire-taut quality of her voice had Noah wondering if he was pushing her too far. "What does that tell you?"

"Stalking is like a long rape." Heat and hatred scorched every word. "He's playing out a fantasy. But Faith's not responding like he'd played out so many times in his daydreams. She turned to you instead of him. He blames her for not cooperating. He feels entitled to his fantasies of her and the perfect life he's planned for them. His goal justifies his behavior. To him it's not harassment, but the natural order of things. I'd say look close.

The guy's unraveling. Or…" Brynna stopped as if catching her breath. "Or maybe you're not dealing with one person."

"Are you saying Faith has two creeps after her?"

"It's something to consider." Brynna blew another long breath, and he could see her sitting at her desk, her little Yorkie on her lap, fingers of one hand raking through the dog's silky coat to soothe her frayed nerves. "You're right to be afraid for Faith. Whoever you're dealing with, he's idealized her. He's made her out to be his perfect woman, his perfect match. If he can't have her, he's going to make sure nobody else will."

THIS WASN'T RIGHT. Something had gone terribly wrong. Who had sent this bomb to hurt his Faith?

He paced the room, touching, straightening, ordering all the things that were already flawless. He relived the horrible nightmare of the fire-seared face over and over again, superimposing Faith's exquisite features over her assistant's shredded skin.

What if Faith had opened the package?

The thought of perfection turning to ghoul

disturbed him on a level that propelled his feet faster and faster around the rectangle of carpet. No longer able to contain the knot of anxiety crushing his chest, he sprinted to his sanctuary.

With a practiced move, he hefted the bicycle off its support on the wall. He checked and rechecked every nut and bolt of his perfectly oiled machine. Helmet, gloves, shoes and he was ready.

Outside, he drank in the cool night air, glad for the missing moon, the lack of stars. Darkness frightened timid souls, but for him, it offered a shroud of solace.

Alone in the dark he pedaled; bombing down the narrow boulder garden he didn't need to see to feel, the hum of chain and gears and wind a sedative. He caught air, landed clean, and slowly the coiled rope of anxiety unkinked.

At the top of a rise, he stood on the pedals and stared at the city lights spread out before him, pretty as a postcard. And in this timeless instant, he realized he could no longer wait.

Whether she was ready or not, he would have to claim his bride.

Chapter Nine

Faith's eyes sprang open as she bolted from a deep sleep to full alert. Her arms windmilled. Her legs kicked out. The blanket holding her hostage flopped to the floor, but the grim dream of smoke and blood and a stealthy black-hooded figure still haunted her. Making out where she was took her a second as the hotel room settled into focus.

Hands braced on the edge of the sofa, she sat still. Every limb in her body ached as if she'd gone a round or two in a boxing ring. A drum was beating in her head.

Safe. She was safe. Away from bombs and fire and blood-seeking reporters. With Noah there, she'd even managed to get some sleep. Had he?

She tightened the sash of her robe and padded from the sitting room to Noah's bedroom. Her gaze strafed the empty room, making her head swim. "Noah?"

She swung back to the sitting room separating their bedrooms. His flow chart of papers no longer graced the floor, but sat in a neat pile on the coffee table, which now stood in its usual space in the middle of the golden carpet rather than against the wall. Had he figured out what kind of sick mind went from leaving flowers to sending bombs?

A rush of water coming from the bathroom ended mid-flow. Toweling his hair dry, Noah peered out the bathroom door, his profile backlit with wispy steam and foggy light, making him look like a dream. The damp waft of the hotel's almond-and-basil soap scented the air. He hadn't yet shaved and the shadow of stubble made her yearn to rub her knuckles across his jaw. Beads of water dotted the muscular lines of his bare chest, ran down his flat belly to the white towel knotted low on his hips, reviving memories of the hot summer night when her lips had traced the same path.

She jerked her gaze away from him, fisting a hand against the vise of pure lust that seized her. The teenage Eagle Scout had filled out into a rock-solid man, but sleeping with him again wasn't an option. Not if she wanted Noah to turn to for an unconditional ear when her soul cracked to pieces. She needed his friendship more than anything. Especially now.

Noah plunked the towel he'd used on his hair onto the bathroom counter. "You're awake."

Clutching the lapels of her bathrobe against the betrayal of her flushed skin, she cleared her throat. "What time is it?"

"Almost nine. I was about to wake you. Detective Rodarte will be here in twenty minutes."

Her eyes widened. "You called him?"

"If we're going to do this, we'll need his help."

He was right. Luring a madman alone was sheer suicide. They would need the detective to put the stalker behind bars. "Thank you for trusting me."

Noah slanted her one of those mysterious half smiles she'd never learned to read. What had she traded for her victory?

He reached to close the bathroom door. "Better get dressed."

She stood and pressed her temples against

the drumbeat in her head that pounded like a dozen marching bands. "I need coffee."

"I'll order room service. Get dressed." The bathroom door clicked shut.

When she came back out of her bedroom fifteen minutes later, wearing black pants, white silk T-shirt and a beige cashmere cardigan, she was glad she'd opted for something comfortable last night in her rush to gather a change of clothes for today. A suit might be more proper for a sting to trap a stalker—one who felt entitled to comment on the appropriateness of her attire—but she needed the balm of softness against her skin to get through the day.

Noah was hunched over the coffee table, green sweater stretched across athletic shoulders, hiding his task from her view until she walked closer. Pieces of two cell phones lay strewn over the tabletop, wire guts exposed. He was using tweezers and looked as if he were performing some sort of organ transplant.

He was intent and content, in his element, tinkering with his gadgets.

A pang of disappointment bumped against her heart. As much as she could use a dose of his friendship on a daily basis, it was too selfish a sacrifice to expect. He couldn't give up Seekers any more than she could give up Byrne's.

Then the bright blue plastic pieces registered and she frowned. "Is that my cell phone?"

"It is. I'm making some improvements and tweaking your GPS so I can find you no matter where you are."

"That's great." His determination to keep her safe touched her. Most people mistook Noah's easy charm for benignness, never realizing that beneath the surface he was an intensely intelligent and focused man.

His deft hands finished putting the pieces of her cell phone back together and he grinned up at her. "I hope you'll still think so when you find out I've linked my cell phone to yours." He flipped her phone open, and the heat in his eyes pinwheeled green into brown. "We're tuned in to each other."

She sat beside him, aware of the pull of his eyes and the tingly energy rippling from his taut body.

"All you have to do is turn on your phone and press the star button." He demonstrated. His phone beeped and his screen lit up with a map that showed her location in Seattle. With another push of a button, her position in the building flashed. "You don't have to dial or talk. Just press the star button, and I'll find you."

His word of honor. She could stake her life on it, on him.

But she couldn't help feeling that somehow her freedom was going to come at a too-high price.

DETECTIVE DAVID RODARTE arrived at the same time as the room service cart. The brown suit over his keg-like body was as wilted today as it had been last night. His lids hung half-mast over his dark pupils as though they were too weary with fatigue to raise full flag. He sat across from Noah in the suite's sitting area, body language as closed as a re-inforced vault door. Noah's plan to insinuate himself into the investigation did not appeal to the detective. "What makes you think that you can do anything better than we can?"

"Because two of the forensics programs your lab uses have The Lovan Group's stamp on them," Noah said. "As does the one I'm beta-testing."

Rodarte shrugged, accepting a cup of coffee from Faith, who needed the task to keep her nerves under control. "So?"

"You know the Lovan programs are the best forensics programs around. Do you know why?"

Rodarte's toothpick rolled around the left side of his mouth, and Noah could almost taste the detective's tobacco craving. "His sister was murdered."

Local boy, driven by guilt, seeks redemption through finding scum like the one that killed his sister. Of course he'd heard the story. Motivation, if there was any. And that motivation was one of Ben's strongest selling tools. "If Bloodhound works like it should, we save time. If it doesn't, you have your techs as backup. Either way, you can't lose."

"I have chain-of-evidence protocol to think about. All I need is for some hell-bent prosecutor to bring up how we let some yahoo taint and alter our evidence—"

"Seekers, Inc. has served as a consultant on cases for the FBI, the U.S. Marshals, the DEA and countless P.D.s. There's precedent both in and out of court for the work we do. All you have to do is sign Seekers on as a consultant. You can take multiple images of every hard drive you confiscated. That leaves an untainted version for your techs. But an analysis with Bloodhound won't change the hash."

"A *consultant* isn't in the budget."

"Do the paperwork, and I'll arrange for a grant in the amount you need to satisfy your bean-counters."

The detective continued to glare at Noah through half-opened eyes.

Noah didn't have time for a long, drawn-out argument. "We can cooperate and pool our resources and skills against a common enemy. Or we can scratch for turf. My way, you can close this case file and move on to the next on your overcrowded docket. Using Bloodhound, I've yet to find a computer I couldn't crack."

Faith planted herself at his side. "We agreed, Noah."

He looked into the roil of her blue eyes, but he wasn't going to give an inch. Not when her life was on the line. And if he got what he needed from his analysis, she'd never have to come anywhere near the bastard, just set up the lure. "We agreed to do things my way.

All I need is a couple of hours to run Bloodhound through the café's hard drive, and I can trace his e-mails back to the source. Then you'll get a chance to draw him out."

Sparks flickered through her eyes. Every crimped finger told him she wanted to walk out the door this instant as bait. "The store reopens on Wednesday."

"It'll be over today." One way or another. It had to be. He had to protect Faith from her own reckless intent.

The detective's coffee breath ground out around the toothpick. "I could haul both of you off to jail for tampering with evidence and interfering with an investigation."

Every muscle in Noah tensed. "Like hell you will. I've been in law enforcement. None of those charges would stick."

He'd like nothing more than to ram the detective's toothpick down his throat. Instead, Noah flashed him a smile. He'd learned this particular one from Falconer right before he swooped in and cut a man off at the knees. And just like Falconer, Noah kept his voice low and ever so polite. "I want to stop this piece of scum before he murders Ms. Byrne." Noah leaned closer to the detective, bumping right up to his personal bubble. "Don't you?" He eased back. "I'd think you'd be all over getting first crack at a technology that could help you get one more dirtbag off the streets."

Faith cleared her throat. "Considering it's my life on the line, and I'm willing to risk it to help you solve your case, Detective, the least you could do is accept a computer expert's help to ease your burden."

The detective chewed on his toothpick and skewered Noah with a hard gaze that said he'd get only one chance to make good on his promise. "Show me what you can do."

ONCE INSTALLED AT A STATION at the bleak and sterile forensics lab, Noah forgot about Faith sitting next to him and Rodarte hanging over his shoulder. All his focus was on the screen in front of him. His computer hummed and whirred. Orchestrating Ben's various programs with dexterous skill, he picked open locked doors and battered down protective walls.

Sniff, crack, open.

He repeated the steps until hard drive after hard drive gave up its secrets. When he was done, he cleared the screen of his computer and pulled up an Internet connection. Cloaked with Ben's Shadow program, he left no footprints as he pried and poked his way along the invisible highway.

Under his practiced fingers, codes and passwords gave way. He followed all the links between Faith and her stalker until they all dead-ended at one single origin point. Once there, he stripped the vaulted files and gained access to the data he sought.

"About time," he muttered.

Smug satisfaction warmed him. The stalker should never have used a flash drive to transport his perverted seduction from home to café. Even going through an intermediary desktop had not saved him.

Noah recovered fragments of word documents, document metadata, link files and other artifacts and was able to derive when each was originally created, when updated versions were tweaked and who had accessed the documents.

This yielded a mother lode of evidence, neatly catalogued with dates, actions and intents, and his heart went sick. This creep was some nut job.

The stalker's electronic diary journaled his

detailed fantasies about Faith, this wonderful thing and the object of his affection. She was his reason to exist, the diarist wrote day after day like a mantra. She had been since she was seventeen and come into his life.

She'd turned him down when he'd asked her for a date soon after they'd met. She'd said their relationship wasn't appropriate. So he'd bided his time, taken every opportunity to show her otherwise, made sure he'd been there when she'd needed someone. He'd shown her care and compassion and companionship. Everything he'd done, he'd done for her.

Scroll forward a decade, and obsession went from words in ether to real-life fulfillment.

The day of her father's heart attack, he'd signed out keys to her office from the security office and invaded her privacy. There he'd found a copy of her house keys and codes and made good use of them in the name of safekeeping. He felt entitled to evaluate her attire, her decisions, her career path, his careful notes scripting his helpful critiques.

He knew how far to go without breaking the law and adroitly pressed the boundaries.

After all, what law could understand a love as pure as his?

With each scrap of attention she gave him, she validated his worth. He needed to possess her.

And Brynna had been right. He couldn't take no for an answer. The more Faith brushed him off, the more frantic he became to hold her.

A new plan, cooked up in the middle of the night, delineated his intent to pour his heart to Faith tonight. If she didn't willingly merge her fate to his, he would hold her until she realized she was his soul mate, meant to live with him forever.

He placed the blame for the need for rash action on Faith. She'd turned to Noah when she should have turned to him.

And if Noah got in the way, he risked paying the ultimate price. The stalker had done it before. He would do it again. For her, he would do anything.

Limbs heavy with fatigue, Noah printed out his findings and handed them to the detective.

The stalker had a name. The stalker had an address.

The stalker had a face.

Yet there was no triumph in the discovery, only the volcanic heat of a temper Noah wrestled back under control.

He could not look at Faith. He couldn't bear to see the pain of another betrayal cloud the sun in her blue eyes. Instead he turned to the detective. "Faith isn't his only victim."

"SHOWTIME, FAITH." Noah, too restless to stay in one place, paced the floor of the police department's small conference room, blurring the neat line of awards and commendations decorating three walls. The bitter coffee he'd consumed all day twitched his muscle into overdrive and turned to acid in his stomach. "Are you sure you're up to this?"

Faith had remained surprisingly composed as Noah had told her stalker's identity and what he'd done to her father. But betrayal was never easy to swallow, and the sharp cut of its pain still slashed the clear blue of Faith's eyes.

Still her jaw was set with determination. She held herself with quiet dignity, cool, distant, untouchable, yet captivating at the same time. "Of course I'm up to this. He hurt my father. I can't believe he's responsible for his heart attack, that he kept poisoning him even in the hospital. How could no one have noticed?"

"It's all about image, Ms. Byrne," Rodarte said. "The staff saw what he wanted them to see."

Noah wished he could do this for her, shelter her from the pain. He crouched beside her, let the subtle scent of her roses-and-linen perfume distract him for a second, and reached for one cold and stiff hand. "You're going to have to relax, or he's going to know something's up."

She nodded, rolling her blue cell phone in one hand, staring at it as if it were some sort of vermin that would bite if she slowed her pace. Seeing her like this hurt more than he wanted to admit.

"You know what you have to do," Noah coaxed.

Her forehead rippled with anxious knots. "Get him to invite me to his house."

"We need to make sure he's there when the officers serve the warrants. Detective Rodarte is borrowing members of the narcotics detail. They're trained to do searches really well. They'll do a center-dump. With his obsessive-compulsive tendencies, he won't be able to stand anyone touching his stuff. That's the best way to manipulate him into wanting—needing—to confess his actions."

With an unknown poison coursing through Philip Byrne's body, speed was of the essence. The more they could pressure the stalker, the faster he would spill his guts.

In Faith's sweet eyes shadows ran rampant. "Are you sure this is going to work? He has to give up the poison."

"He will." Noah glanced over his shoulder at the detective, who watched the scene dispassionately as his toothpick traveled along the closed seam of his mouth. "How long do you need to get your team together?"

"One hour."

Noah turned back to Faith. "Buy us an hour."

Faith nodded, took a deep breath and straightened her already ramrod posture. "Okay, I'm ready."

Her lips trembled, and he wanted to kiss them steady. "He can't hurt you."

With that she dialed, shaking her head until

a smile appeared, looking every inch the efficient manager she was. Noah had never thought he'd cheer the day when her obsession with image would serve her well. A smile could hide so many things—including a lie.

The line picked up and the pulse at her throat kicked up. "Hi, it's me."

She waved a hand at her stalker's question. "I'm fine. I had to drop by the insurance company's office and sign some forms. The police said they'd clear the scene by the end of the day, so we can get moving with the repairs. Look, I have a few things to go over with you regarding finances." She glanced at her watch, and Noah gave her credit for steady nerves. "I have another errand to run, but I can stop by your place around five."

She nodded at the voice on the other end of the call. "When will you be there?"

She motioned for pen and paper and Noah placed both within her reach. She scribbled *7 p.m.?* on the paper and silently questioned the detective.

He nodded.

"Okay," she said, her cheer sounding genuine, "I'll see you then."

She dropped the phone into her lap and

ground a hand into her stomach. "It's all set. He's in the middle of a bike ride, but he should be home within an hour. He's expecting me for dinner at seven."

The detective pushed off the doorjamb. "We'll have you wired and ready to go in at six. We want to catch him off guard. Once he opens the door, we'll bring him down."

Noah squeezed her hand. "You don't have to do this. They can serve the warrants without you."

Faith shook her head. "What if he sees the officers approaching? That could give him a chance to get rid of the poison. I can't risk that. We need to know what he gave Daddy."

Under the conference room's harsh light, color had drained from Faith's face and tension lined the corners of her eyes and mouth. "And I need to see that bastard's face. I need to look into his eyes. I need to ask him why he would want to stalk and kill the people who loved him."

This was a bad idea. Noah couldn't see anything good coming out of Faith facing Griffin. All she'd dredge up was another layer of pain.

He wanted to throw a blanket over her

shoulders, hold her close and steal her home, away from the stress tearing her apart, away from yet another betrayal at the hands of someone she'd loved.

But he'd given her his word.

Chapter Ten

Learning the truth had hurt.

Faith sat in the passenger's seat of the black rental, body bow-tight and ready to fly. Noah turned into Griffin's quiet neighborhood, his tension revving hers. She couldn't see Detective Rodarte or his team, but knew they were all in place, waiting for the next phase of the operation to begin.

Of all the things she'd expected, of all the things she'd prepared herself for, Griffin being her stalker, his having caused her father's heart attack, hadn't even made the list. Despite all the proof Noah had handed her, her mind had a hard time wrapping itself around her stepbrother planning such a long, relentless pursuit. She still couldn't quite believe that he would want to kill her father, simply so she would turn to him for comfort.

And when she hadn't? She shuddered. Why had he thought hurting her would change the texture of her feelings toward him?

Griffin's contemporary home came into view, all angles and gleaming glass, its gray paint melding with the cloudy sky. She'd been to this house only once. It had been mustard-yellow then. Griffin had just put a bid on the place and said he'd wanted her opinion. Spring flowers had exploded in colors from the beds that were now bare. The inside had been free of any furnishings, and she could remember her voice echoing in its emptiness, how cold the plain white walls had felt, and how she'd told Griffin that she'd liked it even though she'd been glad to leave and return to her homey penthouse.

Had he taken her feigned approval as confirmation they were fated to live together in his new house? Had she somehow abetted his delusion and caused him to plan her father's demise?

She wanted to get as far away as possible from Griffin's warped fantasies, not go back into that now-menacing house.

Thinking of Griffin as simply her stalker was somehow more tolerable than admitting the man she'd thought of as her brother had tried to maim her, had tried to murder her father with some unknown poison. A stalker was sick. A stalker was delusional. A stalker wasn't stepping to the drumbeat of reality.

Noah pulled into Griffin's driveway and rammed the car in Park.

Her stomach twisted and clenched.

She'd told herself that the truth was worth the pain. But in reality the truth cut too deeply. Numbness overtook her, encased her body in ice. She reached for Noah's hand, for a scrap of warmth, for his solid strength to bolster her.

He gave her a squeeze of encouragement. "Are you okay?"

"I'm fine." She blinked back the itch in her eyes threatening to dissolve her into tears. She would not cry. Not for Griffin. She wouldn't give him that victory. She gave a small laugh. "I'd so desperately wanted a brother or sister while growing up. When Daddy married Rhea, I was happy to finally have a family."

"I know everything you did to help make him feel part of the family. You were a great sister."

"How did I miss the signs?" Not once when she'd looked into the steel of Griffin's eyes had she read his intent or the fervor of his passion. All she'd ever seen was brotherly concern.

"Why should you have looked for them at all?"

She swallowed hard. Griffin was obviously good at fooling people. "What do you make of his relationship with Tara?"

"All lies."

He'd used Tara's computer to compose his warped love notes. Had he crept out of his fiancée's bed in the middle of the night to send his e-mails? Poor Tara. "I don't like the woman, but she didn't deserve this. Griffin betrayed her, too."

Noah slid closer and wound his arms around her shoulders, his firm body shoring her faltering courage. "After today, he won't be able to hurt anyone."

Irrationally, on the heels of such a close betrayal, she wanted to turn to Noah, to bury herself in him, prove to herself that her fantasies weren't as deluded as Griffin's.

But unlike Griffin, she understood boundaries, knew right from wrong. And she needed someone she could trust now more than ever.

She didn't want to complicate things with Noah, ask for more than he could give.

Noah pulled away from her and reached for the door handle. "Here he comes."

With a trembling hand, she followed suit, exiting the car.

Griffin pedaled down the hilly street, racing against an unseen competitor, not letting up until he reached his driveway.

Pain wrenched in her chest, radiated outward and pulsed like a fresh bruise. *How could you?*

When Griffin saw them standing beside their car, he swung a leg over the bike's saddle, hopped off the still moving bike and came to a halt before them. Sweat darkened the back and chest of his yellow biking shirt.

She forced a smile, dug deep for enthusiasm she didn't feel. "Hey, Griffin. How was your ride?"

He leaned his custom-made bike against his hip and pulled off his gloves. "What's he doing here?"

Noah circled her waist possessively, all smiles and innocence. "I thought you invited us to dinner."

The heat of effort reddening Griffin's face mottled purple as he edged closer to Noah.

Faith stepped between them. "We were just at the hospital visiting Dad, and it was easier to come straight here than double back."

"Well, there's not enough food for three. I wanted some time alone with you, Faith."

"Daddy's getting worse, Griffin. The doctor thinks he might have been poisoned."

Griffin frowned. "Poisoned? How?"

She shook her head, the torment ridging her forehead no act. "We don't know. Can we talk? Inside?"

Griffin nodded, reached into his black bike shorts for his key and headed up the flagstone walkway toward the door. As he shoved the key into the keyhole, Detectives Rodarte and Keyes flanked him. "Hey, what's going on?"

Detective Rodarte held up the warrants. "Griffin Edward Egan, we have a warrant to search your premises and a warrant for your arrest."

"What for?"

"Felony stalking for a start."

Before Detective Rodarte could get the handcuffs on, Griffin lunged at her, hands grabbing for her throat. "How could you do this to me? I love you. We belong together."

"Please, Griffin, tell me what poison you gave Daddy," Faith croaked.

"Me?" Spittle flew as he raged. "How could you even think I'd do something like that?"

With a well-placed nerve block to the shoulder, Noah disengaged Griffin's hold on her. Gasping in breaths, she backpedaled out of the way while the detectives pinned and handcuffed Griffin.

Noah wrapped his arms around her. "Are you okay?"

She nodded, more shocked than hurt.

Griffin fought his restraints. "I want my lawyer."

"It's your right, of course." Detective Rodarte led a balking Griffin inside the house, giving him the rest of his rights. "You'll get your phone call once we're at the station."

Keyes, the rangy cop assigned to pressure Griffin by playing with his bike, talked a mile a minute as he followed Rodarte and Griffin inside, still working on him. "How fast can you go on that thing? How many gears does it have? How much does something like this run? My kid's birthday is coming up. He's got Lance Armstrong dreams."

The rumble of Noah's voice growled in her ear. "You don't have to stay."

She shook her head. "I have to do this. I have to get him to tell us which poison he used and how much."

"The detectives can handle it."

"I can get him to break faster. I want this over." She smoothed her damp palms along the side seams of her slacks, then stepped toward the house.

Two members of the narcotics detail, pressed into service by Detective Rodarte to perform the specialized search, marched into the house. Faith jogged up the stone steps to catch up, Noah glued to her side.

The place was just as Noah had predicted—neat, clean, organized. Sterile, actually, with its blizzard of white-on-white. Shades were drawn to keep prying eyes out, leaving the house cloaked in murky light. The funereal scent of lilies and an undertone of Lysol saturated the house.

Rodarte flipped a switch and an overhead light blasted on, gleaming harshly on the hard, white marble floor. The small entryway opened to a living room on the left and a short hallway to the right. The living room was furnished with a ghoulishly similar grouping as hers, minus the color—as if a decorator had dropped off the furniture and the artist hired to paint it hadn't yet arrived.

How could Griffin possibly think she would want to live in such a tomb of sensory deprivation?

Rodarte jerked Griffin to a halt at the edge of the white carpet. "Where's the poison?"

"There is no poison," Griffin ground out.

Rodarte nodded at the officers. "We'll start here."

The two officers started one at each end of the room, taking all the items out of drawers, cabinets and closets and piling them in the center of the room. Their elongated shadows in the radiant light loomed up the walls like cannibals ravaging a fresh kill. She watched with dark fascination, fervently hoping Noah was right and this center-dump technique would pressure Griffin into confessing what poison he'd used on her father.

Griffin's face contorted into a mask of rage. "Do you have to touch all my stuff?"

"Afraid so."

"There are laws against this."

Rodarte stuck the warrants in front of

Griffin's nose as a reminder. "This says we can."

"You'll pay for everything you damage. My lawyers—"

Rodarte cut him off with a grunt.

A primitive instinct for survival, tapping out a savage rap against her chest, prickled gooseflesh up and down her spine and urged her to run. She couldn't run like a coward. She had to see this through.

The cords in Griffin's neck bulged. "Hey! What are you doing? Be careful with that vase, it's expensive."

Griffin chaffed at the steel bracelets locking his arms behind him, rendering him unable stop the rape of his possessions. "You're going to break that music box."

The officers continued their ordered work. Under the relentless onslaught, a low moan of anguish keened out of Griffin, sounding like a wounded animal, deflating him little by little. "Stop! You have to stop! What are you looking for? I'll tell you, just, please, stop."

"Where's the poison you used on Daddy?" Faith asked. This close, the stink of his sweat swept her back to that night when she'd come home to find *I'm watching you* printed on her television dust.

Griffin's honed gaze slashed her. "If you have any proof I did this, then lay it out."

"I read your journal, Griffin."

His smile twisted sardonically. "I see the way he treats you. I see how much you want him to say *good job*. But he's never going to. Not to you. Not to me. We're never going to be free of him, Faith. Don't you see that?"

"So you decided to kill him?"

"It's right he's hurting the way he's made us hurt. He needs to know the pain. But I didn't do anything to him. There's no poison here."

"He treats you as if you were his own son." This would shatter her father. After all, appearances were everything. Appear to be happy. Appear to be a family. Appear to be in control, always. He wouldn't appreciate the drama that would play out in the papers and on television for all to see as their personal lives were picked apart.

Griffin's upper lip curled. "He treats us like garbage."

"He's dying, Griffin. You have to help me."

"I can't." His voice was soft, almost regretful.

The officers kept on task, moving from róom to room. They came to the second bedroom where Griffin kept all his cycling equipment. Keyes dropped Griffin's prized bike, letting it bounce off the hardwood floor, denting a walnut board, bending a pedal.

Griffin let out a choked growl. "Stop!"

"The poison, Griffin," Noah said. "That's all it takes for this to end."

"Go to hell, Kingsley. She's not yours. You can't have her."

Keyes' busy fingers touched and disturbed tools and equipment. He lifted a cycling helmet off a rack displaying a dozen more. "Wow! Would you look at that! Now that's one rad brain bucket." Keyes turned over the elongated ellipse painted with flames. "Even my boneheaded son would kill to wear something like this."

"Tell us where you're hiding the poison, Egan," Rodarte said.

"There is no poison."

As if Keyes had butterfingers, he let the helmet drop to the floor. "Oops." He picked up the helmet, buffed the scratch with his jacket sleeve, then tossed it on top of the bent bike.

Stress lines cracked Griffin's features. His

chest heaved as if he couldn't get enough air into his lungs. She didn't recognize the animal he was turning into. "This has to stop."

"Just tell us, Griffin," Faith pleaded, "and this can be all over."

"There *is* no poison!"

In the basement, they found the gilded cage he'd built for her. A small ice cream parlor table was set for two. A sheer screen hid a commode. A brass bed piled high with a white feather comforter and silk pillows took up most of the space. A white negligee puddled over the comforter, its diaphanous skirt spread in invitation. A wedding dress of pure white hung in a corner, waiting for its bride. And on the outside of the steel door, a shiny new Yale lock—the better to secure its prisoner inside.

With the sudden fury of a tigress, she lashed out at him. "You can't sneak into someone's home and make them feel unsafe. You can't lock someone in a basement. You can't force them to love you. How could you want to terrorize me that way?"

"No, no, I wasn't terrorizing you. I—"

"Ah, come on, Griffin." Noah shifted his

entire body toward Griffin, his athletic frame ratcheting up to full power, deflecting Griffin's attention from her, a wolf ready to tear her stepbrother to pieces. And though Noah couldn't see her, she sent him her silent gratitude. "You were planning on kidnapping her. You built a cage for her in your basement. You're poisoning her father so you can have her all to yourself."

"She loves me, she just hasn't realized it yet. I'm the only one who can make her happy. She needs me. We share the same goals, the same ideals, the same family. I love her." The last said as if it explained and excused everything.

Noah practically bared his teeth at Griffin. "But you know she doesn't love you. Not that way. That's why you set her up to be picked off by some sex-crazed weirdo. That's why you sent her the bomb. You wanted to scare her into submission."

Griffin's mouth dropped open, and he shook his head so fast it seemed about to twist off his shoulders. "I sent the e-mails, but I swear to God, I didn't set Faith up in the sex chat room or send the bomb. I'd never hurt Faith. Never." His gaze sought Faith's, imploring. "You have to believe me."

"How can I believe you when you won't tell me what you poisoned Daddy with?"

"There is no poison, Faith."

"Your lies are hurting me."

"You got it wrong. I know hurting him would hurt you, and I'd never do anything to hurt you." Griffin's forehead furrowed painfully. "But, Faith…he'll never give you what you want."

"Then that's my problem, not his." And it was, she realized. *Never forget who you are. Make me proud.* She might not have done it the way her father wanted, but she had never forgotten that she was a Byrne and everything she did reflected on the store. She'd let her father's criticism and expectations guide her for far too long. "He doesn't deserve to die."

"He'll kill you. Just like he killed your mother."

Faith gasped. "What are you talking about? My mother died in childbirth."

Griffin growled. "Because he didn't get her to the hospital in time."

"That's enough." Noah grasped her by her shoulders and forced her back up the stairs and into the brisk November air.

She gulped in air to clear the nausea

burning her throat. "He was going to kidnap me. He was going to keep me prisoner. That's why he wanted the extra time today. I'd come to him, making his plan that much easier to carry out. How could he think my father killed my mother? He adored her. Her death changed him."

Noah held her close, staying the trembling of her body. She buried her head in his shoulder. "Griffin won't tell us." She choked back a sob. "He's just going to let Daddy die."

"We'll find the poison with or without his help."

Detective Rodarte yanked Griffin toward the cruiser, waiting at the curb, blue lights swirling against the gray dusk.

Griffin's gaze never wavered from hers as he was folded into the caged backseat of the cruiser, as the door was slammed on his freedom. Like wet cement, whatever crazy form of love he'd ever felt for her hardened into the concrete of hatred.

As the cruiser sped away, in his cruel gaze, she could read his promise. *I'll get you for this.*

Chapter Eleven

"We've run all the tests possible," the doctor informed Faith. His eyes were kind and gentle, and he seemed genuinely worried about her father's condition. "We still don't know what poison was used."

The doctor stood on one foot like a crane, his laptop propped open on the table at the foot of her father's bed. Noah stood behind her, hands on her shoulders. Faith's fingers knitted and reknitted themselves in her lap as she sat next to her father's bed. "There must be something more you can do."

"We'll keep trying."

Noah pointed at the doctor's laptop. "May I?"

The doctor shook his head. "I'm sorry. Patient confidentiality."

"I just need an Internet connection."

The doctor frowned. "What are you looking for?"

"I'm going to plug in symptoms and see what comes up."

"We've already tried that."

"Let me give it a go. Homeland Security has specialized databases that aren't available to the public."

"Then how are you going to get to them?"

"He's a computer expert who consults with law enforcement." Faith reached for her father's hot, dry hand. The convulsion he'd just suffered had left his muscles visibly slack. "Please. My father's getting worse."

Reluctantly, the doctor cleared his screen and ceded his computer.

Noah flexed his fingers and tapped into a database. "Big Brother keeps an eye on all research programs that could give terrorists a new way to spread their hatred. Drugs are one of them. Give me the symptoms."

The doctor consulted the chart. "Increased heart rate, hot, dry skin, rapid pulse and respiration, gradual weakening of muscle, lethargy, convulsions. He seems to have dropped into a deeper coma today."

"Was he on any medication before the heart attack?" Noah asked.

"Cholesterol-lowering pills," Faith said.

The doctor chimed in with the brand name.

Faith jumped up and came to stand next to Noah. "He was getting a lot of headaches before his heart attack and was taking Tylenol like candy."

Noah's fingers blurred over the keyboard and a few minutes later, he turned the screen toward the doctor. "Does this sound plausible?"

The doctor's gaze narrowed, then his brows shot up. "It fits."

He scribbled a note, then shot out the door.

"Harlequinadium Americanus." Faith stared at the picture of a clump of bright red and yellow flowers. Too pretty to be so harmful. "I've never heard of it."

"It's a weed. The sap is thick, almost like a cream, and poisonous. It's deadly long-term, but it takes repeated dosing to get there. If that's it, they can treat it. Your father should pull through without too much damage."

"Where did it come from?"

"It's pretty much extinct now due to en-croaching development, but it used to grow near water like lakes and ponds in the northern states and Canada."

Faith shook her head. "Then how would Griffin get hold of it or get my father to take it? Are you sure you have the right poison?"

"Nature's Boon Laboratories has found a way to propagate *harlequinadium* cheaply and easily and use the sap for medicinal purposes. Look who owns the lab."

"Dr. Terrence Widrick." Her gaze sought his. "Tara's father. That's why Griffin chose her."

Noah nodded. "The doctor will order the drip antidote, and your father should be back to his old, crotchety self in no time."

A sense of both relief and sadness coursed through her. "I know Daddy hurt you terribly. But he wasn't always this way. Before I was born, everyone says, he was a warm, loving man."

She shrugged, hugging herself. "And then, I took my mother away from him. Gran said it was like watching a fire die out the way life burned out of him."

"Your mother's death isn't your fault."

"I know." On a logical level, anyway. But in her heart she'd always felt as if she owed her father something for taking the woman he loved away from him.

She glanced at the helpless form of her father and suddenly understood his distance.

Her father's love was conditional, because he'd loved too much and lost. Griffin's love was twisted, because he'd never been loved enough. His mother and father had constantly traveled when he was young, and he was raised by a series of nannies he'd said were cold and harsh. And her father had continued that apathetic tradition. By the time Faith had come along, hungry for a brother, he'd taken her attention for something it wasn't.

The only one who'd ever loved her as she was, the only person she could count on was Noah.

She hugged her arms in close.

Noah. She didn't know what to do about Noah.

She stole a look at him. His gaze caught hers and a tornado of emotions hit her, uprooting all logic as it spun inside her, the rush of sensations threatening to suffocate her. The power of those feelings was so strong it hurt. Her fingers grafted an unconscious coop against her heart.

She loved him, she realized, the way that Griffin had wanted her to love him. Friendship wasn't enough. It never had been.

She swiveled back to her father, fearful that Noah could read the nakedness of her improper desire.

It was the stress, she rationalized. She was grateful for Noah finding the stalker and arranging his capture. For saving her father's life. That was no reason to turn him into the romantic hero Griffin had wanted to be. Indulging in impossible fantasies was wrong. Today was a blaring example of why.

A nurse came in to start the IV drip that would counteract the poison weakening her father's body. An hour later, he was resting more comfortably, his vital signs dropping back to the normal range and renewed health pinkening his skin.

Noah had wanted to take her home, but she'd insisted she had one last stop to make before she could put the whole mess behind her. So here they stood in front of Byrne's. Seeing the windows darkened like this was strange. Traffic on a Monday night wasn't the thickest, but there were always shoppers strolling the aisles.

Noah stepped behind her and took the key from her hand. "This can wait till morning. I'll make you a nice meal while you soak in a tub full of bubbles."

"That sounds like heaven." She couldn't remember eating anything since the hurried muffin for breakfast. "But this will only take a minute. I need to check on the store."

The police had finished their investigation and released the scene a few hours ago. First thing in the morning a crew would arrive to rip out every trace of the bomb damage.

Though Faith had seen the damage the bomb had wreaked, a fresh wave of shock hit her as she entered her office. The bitter smell of wet charcoal assaulted her nose. Water, ash and foam had created a blackened mess on her desktop that had oozed down the side like puss from a wound. Sergio's blood had darkened on the carpet, leaving a ghost image of his trauma behind.

Everything would need to go. She'd need to order fresh paint, new carpets, new furniture. In a day or two, everything would be back to normal—as if nothing had happened.

She frantically worked at the knots tying her throat.

Except for Sergio. He was in for a long, painful recovery.

The thick layer of guilt made pulling air into her lungs painful.

She was tired, so tired. She wanted a hot bath, Noah's promised meal and sleep. A full night with no threat of intruders, no fear of being stalked. No dying father. No betraying brother.

She narrowed her gaze in an attempt to focus.

She would set up a temporary office in the conference room. For now, her priority was the store's reopening on Wednesday. If she concentrated on that one goal, she could hang on to her sanity. A ragged laugh escaped her. Was that how her father had rationalized the long hours at work after her mother's death?

Like father, like daughter? Why not? Survival 101. Put Byrne's first.

Curiosity seekers would no doubt flock to see if any trace of the tragedy remained. What was it about other people's troubles that had such magnetic attraction?

Vultures.

She'd have to call in extra staff to handle the

excess foot traffic for the first few days. After that, she hoped it was the good deals that would bring them back and not the morbid fascination with a bomb wrapped in a present.

And then, just like that, Focused Faith snagged on Noah's intense gaze and disappeared.

All that loss. All for what?

In his eyes she caught empathy, a swirl of sadness, the heat of desire. He moved toward her until they were almost touching, his wonderful hazel eyes keeping her captive. "Close your eyes."

"Why?"

"Shh. Just do it."

A twinge of trepidation vibrated down her spine as he took her hands.

"Imagine this office as you want it," he said, his voice a hypnotist's metronome. "What does it look like?"

"Well, there's the glass desk and the computer and the chrome shelves. Clean lines and no clutter."

"No. If you could make it any way you wanted. Never mind your father's taste. Never mind what everyone's idea of what a department store manager's office should look like.

When you see your office, decorated by you, just as you want it, what do you see?"

She took in a breath, closed her eyes and played along. She couldn't help the smile when the first picture popped into her head. "There's this antique desk I saw a few months ago. I loved that everything was within reach. And there's a chair I saw online that's this bright raspberry color. Dad would think it would be more suited for a kindergartner—"

"It's your imaginary office. You father has no say."

In the space of her imagination she sat on that raspberry chair at the antique desk and looked around at the walls. "I'd paint the walls pale green—like you see in the spring on new flowers."

She was caught up in the game now, seeing all the things that would make her office feel like home. "I want lush carpet I can sink my toes into. And these amazing photographs of flowers I saw at a gallery a couple of blocks up from here."

Noah's voice rumbled in her ear. "How does it make you feel?"

Head on his shoulder, his heartbeat in tune with hers, she examined the strange, floating sensation inside. "Happy. It makes me feel happy."

He kissed the top of her head and it warmed like a blessing. "Okay. It's done."

"It's a nice dream." She reluctantly lifted her head from his shoulder.

"Keep your eyes closed."

He kissed her racing pulse at the hollow of her neck and the room started to spin. He kissed her lips, so tenderly, savoring as if they had an eternity. She felt suspended in time, all thoughts pushed out of her mind. The tension of the day melted away. Griffin's betrayal disappeared. Her father and Sergio's bodies, each helpless under hospital sheets, vanished. The charred remains of her office evaporated.

Then when she was nothing more than clay in his hands, he let her envision her dreams, the picture of the color and life of her imagined office firing her brain with possibilities.

He held her close, one arm scooped gently around her waist. His mouth tickled her ear and he whispered, "Let's go home."

And when they came out into the streets, neon lights giving false cheer to the drizzle of

rain, she understood. Her stalker was caught.
Her father would recover. She was safe.

Noah was saying goodbye.

Chapter Twelve

Faith's apartment was warm and inviting, the faint glow of a light on a timer in the living room welcoming them home. Noah dropped the grocery bags they'd stopped to buy in the kitchen. Then, out of habit, he checked every room.

When he returned to the kitchen, the sight of Faith looking lost tore at him. "Are you okay?"

She grabbed the kettle and hung on to it as if she wasn't quite sure of its function. "I can't believe this is happening. Part of me just wants to run and hide, even now that Griffin's been caught."

"It's not a sign of weakness, you know."

"I doubt my father would agree with you." Faith jabbed the water on, filled the kettle and set it on the stove, then leaned her backside against the counter, watching him, her eyes pinched. "You're leaving, aren't you?"

He had to, for both their sakes. Before he did something unwise, like tell her he loved her. He'd seen her with her father at the hospital. She'd always be Philip Byrne's daughter first, no matter who she married. With Faith, duty to family came before everything else. He couldn't ask her to change.

The weight of responsibility pressed on him, and he felt disloyal as he unloaded the chicken breasts and broccoli and new potatoes, wanting more than he had a right to. Especially after a day like today. "You're safe now."

"For how long?"

"It's Griffin's first offense." Noah shrugged and stuffed strawberries and cream into her bare fridge. Despite Griffin's protests to the contrary, hard evidence pointed to her stepbrother's deteriorating mental balance. He'd sent the present. He'd used Tara to gain access to a controlled substance that would be hard to trace. And he'd planned to hold Faith prisoner until she loved him back.

For that alone, Griffin should spend the rest of his days behind bars as far as Noah was concerned. But he wouldn't. "If they add criminal threatening to the felony stalking charge, he's looking at eighteen months. Two years at most."

Noah slammed the fridge door harder than he'd meant. He wouldn't let himself think about what would happen when Griffin was released from prison. By then, her father would be back in charge. He'd protect her. And Noah knew from experience the reach of Philip Byrne's power to protect his only child.

Faith reached into the cupboard for two mugs and dropped a tea bag in each. "That's something anyway."

"I'll beef up your security system, and hire a bodyguard to stay with you until Griffin's trial is over."

"You think he could get away?"

"No." No way Griffin would make bail. Noah had seen to that. But it didn't hurt to be prepared. At least it would ease his guilt once he was back home. "I wouldn't leave you if I didn't think you'd be safe."

The kettle shrieked and Noah snapped the burner off, strangling the whistle mid-blow. Then he hunted around for a cutting board and a knife.

"A bodyguard's not necessary." She

stretched a hand out to stay his search. Her eyes glittered like blue topazes. "I'd rather have you."

His yearning for her had been simmering since he'd seen her waiting for him in the airport lobby. The best thing for him to do was to start on dinner, pretend he couldn't see a mirror of his need in her eyes. Instead he stepped toward her, crowding her, his arms caging her against the counter. "You know I can't stay. I have to get back to my job."

"I know." But her eyes said, *why not?* Then she answered her own unspoken question. "You need your job as much as I need mine."

Honor, loyalty, commitment. How could he resent in her the very principles by which he lived? He pushed a stray lock of her hair behind her ear, the softness of it weakening his resolve. "It's everything I've worked toward. Freedom to run things my way. Making a difference."

"That's always been important to you." There was something both edgy and bleak in the tone of her voice. "And you're not a city type of guy. Too much chaos. I know how much you like your peace and quiet."

"I like cities just fine. I grew up in Boston, remember? You're not a country girl. I've always known that. Your father and the store come first."

She drew in a long breath, shaking her head. "It's not that they come first, it's that they're part of my DNA—like my eyes and my blond hair. I can't change—"

"I know." A dull ache thrummed alongside his heart for all he wanted, all he could never ask of her.

"Still…I wish you could stay." And he could read the fervor of that wish in the widening pupils of her eyes.

He skimmed a longing finger over her freckles and pushed away from her. "We're not good for each other, shortcake."

She grabbed his wrists. "You're my best friend."

He leaned forward until his lips almost touched hers. "I want to be more than friends, Faith." He could no longer deny it. "Like before."

She shivered, fueling his desire. "I remember. Kiss me, Noah."

Kiss her? He groaned. Did she realize what she was asking? Was he wrong? Was she ready to break free of her father's tight rein? "The last time I kissed you, things didn't end so well."

"I'm not a teenager anymore. I can make my own decisions."

He gave her the lightest of kisses, and that only served to torch all the feelings he'd capped tight. "Faith..."

She kissed him back with an elemental thirst that made him dizzy.

Coming up for air, he pressed his full arousal against her belly. "I want you more than I've ever wanted anything. It's killing me."

"I know the perfect cure." Her eyes, dark with desire, left no ambivalence as to her wishes. She released his wrists and her hands climbed up his chest. Her fingers raked into his hair, awakening smoldering tinder after tinder of dormant desire.

"You can't go," he choked out in warning. "I can't stay."

"I know."

He focused on the sweet taste of her mouth. Slow. He would take it slow. Enjoy every kiss, every touch as if it were his last. His hands skimmed her arms and pushed aside the soft cashmere of her sweater. The hammer of a pulse pounded through his head, blocking all thoughts, the shrill of alarm nothing but a distant echo.

His hands cupped her breasts over the silk of her T-shirt, thrilling at the bloom of her nipples under his thumbs. She sucked in a breath and arched her back, inviting his deeper touch. That he could have this effect on her only served to sharpen his hunger for her.

Wrong time, his mind tried to warn him again.

But he wanted her, just as he'd wanted her that summer, with a fierceness that defied all logic.

And look what that got you.

The bad memory of Philip Byrne's anger sliced into him. But the haze of desire softened the remembered blow.

It was different now. They were both adults, free to choose who they loved. And they both knew going in there was no future.

He deepened his kiss, asking more of her, letting her eager response feed his excitement.

He wanted that blind tumble over the edge of reason, that pitch into sheer insanity. He wanted *her.* Even if only for tonight.

As if she'd read his mind, Faith smiled that wicked smile that had taken him prisoner so long ago. With the flair of a temptress who knew exactly the havoc she was causing, she flattened her hand along the ridge of his erection and rubbed down its length. The last remnant of caution was lost in the mad roar of his blood.

IT HAD BEEN TWELVE YEARS since they'd last made love. Faith didn't expect the same fireworks, the same explosion of desire and sheer lust. They were adults now, not hormone-driven teenagers. But when Noah pulled her into his arms and when his firm lips met hers, heat fired into every cold cell of her body. The curves of her body, fitting so well against the hard planes of his, shocked her with need so deep and so volcanic that she kissed him back with all the urgent passion she'd locked away so long ago.

She wanted, needed to touch him, all of him, as she had on that one perfect night. She wanted him out of his clothes and lying beside her, skin to skin, his body moving into hers, filling her, filling the empty hollow inside her that threatened to engulf her.

Refusing to let each other go, they moved in a frantic dance toward her bedroom, kicking off shoes. The zipper of his Dockers gave way under her greedy fingers. She pushed the stiff material off his hips, taking his shorts along for the ride. The soft wool of her slacks slinked down her legs, puddled on the floor.

Insatiable kiss met insatiable kiss. Fevered touch kindled fevered touch. Unquenchable hunger inflamed unquenchable hunger.

His hands glided along her hips, skimmed to her inner thighs. One thumb brushed against the scrap of silk stretched across her most sensitive place. She sucked in a breath, the searing rush of her response startling her.

She lost her balance, tumbling him backward. He landed heavily on the office chair at her desk, taking her with him. Laughing, she dropped onto his lap, straddling him.

His hard erection pulsed against her, hot and urgent, and suddenly the bedroom seemed much too far away. Her hands clasped around his shoulders, her mouth dipped to plunder his, her chest pressed against his, wanting nothing more than to melt right into him.

Noah understood her in a fundamental way. He'd listened to her and supported her over the years. He'd never put down her drive to make Byrne's a success the way Heath had. They'd once shared hopes and dreams, fears and worries, bodies and souls under a moonlit sky.

Was she wrong to want that magic back? Could they somehow make it work for longer than a night?

She yanked his sweater over his head, ripped the shirt right off his chest. She'd get him a new one in the morning. With a ravenousness she didn't recognize, she tasted the heat of his skin, the tang of his musk.

He pulled her T-shirt off, eased his way down her body, hands gliding along her skin, igniting spark after spark of yearning as he pressed her closer. With one nimble tweak of his fingers, the clasp of her bra sprang open, offering her breasts to his eager mouth. His tongue tormented her aching nipples, and her body trembled like an earthquake. She fisted her hands into his hair and willed the tremors to quiet.

She was breathless, desperate for this night to last. "Wait, wait, wait."

But he didn't. The silk of her underwear shredded under his intent fingers.

He lifted her hips until he could impale himself into her and his groan rumbled against her heart. For a moment time stood still. She couldn't move. She couldn't think. She couldn't breathe. Then air rasped back into her lungs in pure licks of fire. She wrapped her arms around his neck, shifting her hips forward, throwing her head back, wanting, needing more of him.

The rhythm of their lovemaking pounded to the hammer of her heart and the thunder shaking through her body rolled on and on. She wanted to stay at this point of perfection forever.

In his arms, she'd found a place beyond memory. She'd found a place of warmth and pleasure and love. And she didn't want to give it up.

Tears dammed her throat.

I love you, Noah.

The thought brought with it a surge of fear. She stared into Noah's desire-darkened eyes, at the beautiful pinwheels of green and brown rimming his dilated pupils, at the very depth of his soul open to her, and a terrible, aching emptiness iced the edges of her heart.

Please, Noah, don't leave me again. I couldn't stand the pain.

IN THE GRAY LIGHT OF DAWN, they nestled under the covers of the blue duvet of her bed, Faith's head resting in the crook of his shoulder, her arm over his chest. Noah loved the feel of her hands on him, the smell of sex on her skin, the way she fit the length of his body as if she'd been made just for him.

A pinch of melancholy smarted for all the lost years. And he couldn't help anticipating the moment the bubble would burst. He didn't want to face reality. Not yet.

Faith lifted her head and studied his frown. "You're not sorry, are you?"

"Hell, no." He traced the sweet sprinkling of freckles across her nose with the tip of a finger. He wanted to remember her like this, hair mussed, cheeks pink, blue eyes soft and vulnerable. "But it makes things more complicated."

Faith snuggled back onto his chest. "We

can work things out. Could you find a job here in Seattle?"

His fingers skated up and down the bumpy tract of her spine. "I don't think finding a job is the issue."

"Then what is?"

"When Daddy calls, you answer, even if it's not in your best interest. You're twenty-eight. You run a multimillion-dollar business. You shouldn't be letting anyone tell you who you can and can't love. I'm not willing to come third in line after your father and the store."

She sat up, holding the sheet across her breasts like a shield. "I love you, Noah. I never stopped. I want to be with you. I want a life with you. But you can't ask me to choose between you and my obligations to my father and to Byrne's. That's not fair."

He wrapped a loose strand of her blond hair around his finger. "I'm a realist, Faith. There's always going to be another emergency at Byrne's, another call from your father. I want to move forward with my life. I want a family. Children." Wanted them more than he'd ever realized. "I'd like to do both with you. Do those priorities fit anywhere in your ten-year goal plan?"

"You know they do. But…" Her eyes pleaded for understanding. "I owe him. Don't you understand?"

"Your mother died giving birth to you, but you didn't cause her death. Your grandmother should never have insinuated as much. Your father's emotional cave-in isn't your problem, either."

Philip Byrne's over-the-top reaction twelve years ago did make bizarre sense now that Noah understood his loss. In Philip's mind, Noah could have taken his daughter away from him forever. If she'd accidentally gotten pregnant, Philip would have risked having to watch her die the way he'd watched his wife die.

Faith's eyes brimmed with apology. "He's sick right now. For the first time in my life, he needs me."

"I can't wait for you forever, Faith." He'd seen how one-sided goals and ambitions could poison a relationship.

His parents were happy now, but Noah could remember all the nights his mother had kept dinner warm for his father and then thrown it out uneaten, all the nights she'd cried herself to sleep alone, because business had come first.

I'm making a life for you and the kids, Rosalyn. I'm giving you all the things I never had.

But it's you we want, Roger. Can't you see that?

It wasn't until the big cancer scare ten years ago that his father had realized that he'd missed his children growing up, that his wife had one foot out the door. And that if something didn't change drastically, he'd lose all he'd sought to protect. That's when he'd started grooming his children to take over. But Noah had wanted none of it. He'd already figured out work wasn't everything, maybe not even the biggest thing.

But Faith hadn't.

And Noah couldn't settle for third place in her life.

"I can't make this kind of decision now." She placed a hand over his heart, and he could feel her warmth brand the cold knot of regret lodged in his chest. "Not when my father's in the hospital. Please. After he's released, we'll talk. We'll work something out."

Every word, every expression bore the stamp of sincerity.

But Noah got it. He got her. She loved him, but she loved her father more. Nothing would change. He finally got it, heart, mind and soul, that she would never be his.

THEY'D PHOTOGRAPHED and printed him like some damned criminal. He'd had to spend the night in a jail cell. He'd had to resort to draping toilet paper over the cot to protect himself from the filth. And now they were processing him like cattle at a slaughterhouse, along with every other thief, rapist and killer in town. With the drop of a hammer by a judge on the other side of a video camera, his fate was sealed. He was going to be tried on felony stalking charges.

He snorted. Since when had love become a felony?

"Griffin Edward Egan!" some petty uniformed clerk shouted.

Griffin stood. "Here."

"Your bail's been posted."

Two hundred and fifty thousand bucks, but it was worth every penny.

A buzzer zapped the lock on the door and it clinked and clanged open. His steps echoed in the bad acoustics that matched the bad lighting.

"You're to report to this address for your psych evaluation at nine a.m. tomorrow morning," the clerk said, the rote of the task giving the same weight to every syllable. "Here's your court date."

Ignoring the continuing torrent of instructions, Griffin accepted both sets of orders, but had no intention of fulfilling either. By the time any of those dates came up, he'd be gone, and Faith would be his.

Or she'd be dead.

Chapter Thirteen

By five o'clock, Noah was on his way to the airport, and the salvage crew had emptied her office to its bare bones and left. She'd gone over every inch of the retail floor and everything was set for the next morning's ten a.m. opening. And Marlon, the bodyguard Noah had hired, was driving Faith crazy as he sat watching her from the corner of the conference room.

Restless, she clicked on the news. Her family's story played out on the flat-screen television hanging on the wall as if it were someone else's drama. None of it felt real. She blasted the screen back to black.

She couldn't believe Noah had gone. That she'd let him go. She focused back on her file. They'd work it out. Somehow. Once her father was out of the hospital, she'd fly to

New Hampshire and they'd talk. She'd prove to him that, although Byrne's was important, her father didn't control every aspect of her life. She had a right to a family and children of her own. How else would Byrne's pass on to the next generation? And she wanted that family, those children with Noah. No one else understood her the way he did.

They'd said their strained goodbyes on the sidewalk in front of her condo building. He would drive the rental back to the airport and her new bodyguard would drive her to Byrne's in his reinforced car. Overkill, now that Griffin was behind bars, but Faith couldn't manage enough energy for an argument.

Wind buffeted the large windows with angry fists, and even though every overhead fluorescent light was burning bright, a low-grade hum of anxiety made sitting still almost impossible.

Faith didn't want to go home, where too many fresh memories of Noah and the love they'd made haunted her condo, reminding her of what they could have if she renegotiated her relationship with her father. But she couldn't think about that now. Her father would need weeks to recover well enough for her to start changing the rules.

She couldn't stay here either. She'd never experienced the store so quiet. Even late at night there was usually a pleasant buzz of comforting noises. Now, it was as if death had moved in and was taking root. She fumbled under the table for her heels, gathered her files and stuffed them in her briefcase. "Am I allowed to feed you?"

Marlon, massive and mean looking, stood up and his face cracked into a smile, giving him the appearance of a benevolent genie. "Three times a day is best."

She gave a small laugh, slipped on her jacket and led him toward the elevator. Red for courage, she'd thought this morning as she'd dressed. She didn't feel courageous, though, just a shell over a cold, empty core. Just like her father. She swallowed a bitter snort. Definitely an example she needed to break.

She wanted this crazy work, yes, but she also wanted love and laugher, someone with whom to share the trials and triumphs. Someone like Noah, who thought nothing of jumping into an airplane and flying three thousand miles just because she was scared.

She sniffed at the backlog of tears pushing to flood. "How does Thai sound? I have a craving for drunken noodles."

"I can eat anything."

That she could believe. By sheer force of his size, he could overpower anything short of King Kong. Keeping all that muscle on had to require a mass of food. "There's a place a couple of blocks over. The walk'll do me good."

Maybe the cold wind would numb her brain and she could forget about Noah.

"I'd prefer to drive."

She jabbed the down button, impatient now to get out of here as quickly as possible. "I really need to move and air my head."

He gave it some thought, then nodded. "We'll walk."

She'd waited a lifetime to take over operations of Byrne's and her goal was almost within reach. Why didn't it taste as sweet as it should have? She closed her eyes tight. Noah, of course. Could she give up her family's legacy? Could she make a clean break and start over? Was love enough or would bitterness and resentment eventually taint their relationship?

New Hampshire, as fond as her memories were of her summers there, would make her restless with so much empty time to fill. She needed the frantic pace, the constant challenge. But, God, she would miss Noah, miss him like crazy. There had to be a way to give them both their everything.

The elevator door binged and the brass doors whooshed open. She stepped in. As she turned around to face forward, Marlon's eyes bulged, his mouth gaped in a silent scream and his body dropped like an empty sack.

As the doors started to close, a blur of black energy burst into the elevator, bloody knife's steel glinting in the elevator's light. The doors jolted closed. The car started to move, gears grinding. The face swam to clear, the eyes of a killer inches from hers.

Griffin pressed the knife's point against the tender flesh at the base of her throat. "Now I have you all to myself."

NOAH GRITTED HIS TEETH. He was supposed to have taken off over an hour ago. "When do you think the airport will reopen?"

The underpaid dispatcher somehow managed to keep a smile on as she repeated the same information to irate pilot after irate pilot. "The crosswinds are too dangerous right now to allow any takeoffs. As soon as they abate to safe levels, we'll let you know."

He slapped both hands on the counter and pushed back. The weather delay wasn't her fault and complaining wasn't going to get him an earlier takeoff time.

He sat in the lounge, watching the wind sock blow straight out at a ninety-degree angle to the runway, dust and debris skipping over the tarmac like snow. Banks of clouds stirred around Mount Rainier, a mirror of his frustration.

He shoved open his laptop, working and reworking his flight plan. He could still make it home tonight and be at his desk first thing, ready for the morning briefing. Falconer had a new case and was anxious for input. That would keep Noah busy and he wanted to be so busy he wouldn't have time to think. And that was the crux. What he was really desperate to do was avoid thinking about Faith.

He loved her. She loved him. Could they make it work? She'd asked for time. But he had a sinking feeling it would make no difference. That Faith could never quite make a personal relationship her priority. Philip Byrne had too powerful a hold on his daughter.

Noah didn't want to give up all he had at Seekers just to fall to the bottom of Faith's busy agenda.

He slammed the top of his laptop shut. Faith had taken up so much of his heart for so long. All he could think of was her—the roses-and-linen smell of her, the sugar-and-spice taste of her, the silk-and-satin feel of her. The way she made him feel light and content with just a smile. The way her body responded to his was sweeter than any music.

But it wasn't enough.

He'd meant what he'd told her. He didn't want to play third string. He'd seen how that could slowly kill love. He never wanted to grow to hate her, the way his mother almost had his father. And he wasn't willing to put his life on hold forever while she found the courage to defy her father.

He scrubbed a hand over his face, wiping at the fatigue, then put on his glasses. Outside the window, the wind scoured the country-side clean. If he left Faith alone, would she have the strength to stand up for herself? Or was he throwing the lamb back to the wolf?

"FORGET ABOUT ME, BITCH?" Griffin's face was contorted with such anger that for a moment Faith's heart stopped. Was he going to kill her the way he'd attempted to kill her father? Panic gushed, scattering her thoughts.

"Cat got your tongue?"

She shook her head too fast, felt the blade of his knife nick her skin, sting.

Griffin's gaze fixed her throat, as if the spilling of her blood fascinated him. He added a second small cut, then a third. "I'll make you remember. This time you won't forget me."

"I remember you, Griffin." She gulped. "I remember all the good times we had."

"Shut up!"

Her heart stampeded. *Stay cool, stay calm. It's your only chance to stay alive.*

And God knew she'd pretended often enough to look composed when she'd been anything but. Chalk one up for Gran and Daddy's training.

But this was different. This wasn't a teenage rebellion or a boardroom blunder. Her life was on the line.

And suddenly the store, running it, protecting her legacy didn't seem so important.

How could she have told Noah she needed more time? How could she have allowed the one person she loved most to walk away from her? So New Hampshire wasn't Seattle. So what? She had brains, didn't she? She had skills. She could start a new business there and have Noah. They could both have their everything. Why had she given him up so easily?

Griffin watched her with calculated attention, as if he was seeing her for the first time and didn't like the picture he saw. "How cool and superior are you going to look when I hack your guts all over your precious store?"

Her throat worked as she tried to squeeze out her voice. "If it's the store you want, Griffin, you can have it. No questions asked."

"I don't want the damn store. I never wanted the store. I wanted you."

Pulse beating a frantic race, she swallowed hard. "You don't have to do this, Griffin. Please."

Griffin's eyes burned with wild fever. "Do what?"

"Hurt me."

He tipped his head, the smooth velvet of

his voice chilling. "You know what I'd like to do to you?"

Nausea twisted in her stomach at the thought. "You're my brother. I love you. You don't want to hurt me."

The knife's tip skated from side to side, scratching but not breaking the skin above her throbbing jugular. "I'd like to punch your face in until it's a bloody pulp." The lover's sensuality vaporized, turned brutal. "See how you enjoy going through life like an ugly troll."

"I wouldn't, Griffin. You know that. You know me better than anyone." Except Noah. And she'd let him go as if that intimate knowledge didn't mean anything.

Griffin shifted the knife and sank the bloody tip into her loose hair, pushing it back, exposing more of her neck to his blade. She sucked in a breath. "That's right. I know you. I know everything about you. How could you give yourself away to that loser Boy Scout? You're nothing but a whore."

"We were kids. I didn't know you then."

"You're used to getting everything your way, aren't you? You played with me, Faith. You let me believe you loved me—"

"As a brother."

His gaze narrowed and hardened. "As your soul mate."

Don't argue. It's not going to get you anywhere. "I'm sorry I gave you that impression. I was so happy to finally have a brother."

The first-floor button chimed. A bolt of terror zigzagged down her spine. If she had any chance to get away, she had to catch Griffin off guard.

His gaze shifted to the opening door.

Now.

Gaze never leaving his face, she slammed her briefcase into his Adam's apple. The blow shoved his head back. The doors opened, and he fell onto the landing, wheezing and gagging. She reached inside the purse still hanging from her shoulder and grabbed her phone.

Out, she had to get out.

Heart banging, legs churning, chest burning, she raced toward the store's closest exit across the darkened retail floor. If she could crash through the doors, alarms would go off everywhere. Breath chugging, she cut through accessories and into misses. How long did it take to fuel and ready a jet? She flipped her phone open and thumbed the star button, praying with all her might that Noah hadn't taken off yet.

Before she could dial 911 for good measure, her knees caved, her feet were swept out from under her and her phone went flying.

"MR. KINGSLEY?"

Noah looked up from his concentrated analysis of the file Falconer had sent him. Not that he'd absorbed a word of it.

The dispatcher smiled. "The winds have shifted enough that we will be allowing air traffic to resume in half an hour. You may start your preflight check."

Relief gushed. *Finally.* In no time he'd be heading east, too busy keeping his jet airborne to think about Faith. "Thanks."

He gathered his bags and jogged to the gate. Just as he was about to push through the door, his phone beeped.

Ignore it. Just move on.

But the frantic notes beat against his brain.

He jarred to a stop, a sense of foreboding icing his veins, and fumbled for his phone. The screen flashed *SOS*. From the phone he'd rigged for Faith. She'd pressed the panic button. He dropped his duffel bag and dialed Faith's number, but it kicked straight to voice mail. "Faith, it's me. If you get this message, call me. I'm coming, you hear. You hang on."

He tried the bodyguard and got no answer.

He punched in 911.

"What's your emergency?" the operator inquired.

"I just got a call from Faith Byrne at Byrne's Department Store. She's in trouble. Her bodyguard isn't responding and neither is she. Send someone."

He answered the operator's questions, but refused to stay on the line after he'd given all the information he had. He tried Faith again, and again got her voice mail. He tried the bodyguard with the same results.

Without a thought, Noah spun around, swept up his duffel and ran to the rental counter. A gray-haired matron in a company-logo vest opened her mouth to speak, but Noah cut her off. "I need a car. *Now*. It's an emergency."

She peered down at her computer. "We have a Focus and a Fiesta left. The wind, you know."

"Give me the closest one."

"How long do you need it for?"

"A couple of hours."

She stared at him over the top of her glasses.

"I'll pay the full day's rate." Geez, could she make this drag on any longer?

With the speed of a turtle crossing a highway, the paperwork finally dribbled out of the printer. "If you'll sign here, here and here."

Noah scribbled his signature, impatience bubbling to the surface. He couldn't wait any longer. He flung his credit card at the clerk and grabbed the key from her hand. "I'll be back."

Outside, the force of the wind slapped him off balance. He tucked in and sprinted toward the rental lot.

He put a call through to Detective Rodarte. "Where's Griffin Egan?"

"He posted bail."

Noah cringed. "How could you cut him loose?"

"Not my choice."

"He didn't have enough cash on hand to meet the bail." Noah had made sure of that.

"It was paid by Tara Widrick."

Noah swore and yanked the rental's door

open. "You need to get to Byrne's right now. Faith sent me an SOS, and she's not responding. Neither is her bodyguard. Griffin's got her. And he's not planning on playing nice. Not when he blames her for his arrest."

"I'm on my way."

Dusk leached the color from the sky, leaving a gray backdrop, punctuated with garish neon that blurred and smeared as he sped down I-5. Wind whipped the lightweight rental all over the highway. Desperate for a hole in the traffic, he cut off a semi. An air horn blared behind him.

Rain started as he veered down the Fourth Avenue ramp without slowing down. Buzzing through a red light, he hooked onto Yesler. Growling at the maze of unfamiliar one-way streets, he wound around until his destination was in sight.

"No, God, no." The car bucked a protest as he braked to a stop at the ring of trucks blocking the street and hit the sidewalk running.

Byrne's was in flames.

Chapter Fourteen

"You're coming with me," Griffin's rough voice rasped in her ear.

Before Faith had a chance to clear her foggy mind from her fall, Griffin yanked her by the hair and dragged her toward the holiday display in the misses department— away from the windows, from possible help. Moving thickly, her limbs heavy as if she were underwater, she stumbled forward, one shoe on, one shoe off.

Only the murky fixtures lit the store. Foot traffic outside would lessen with each passing hour. No one would notice anything wrong. Not until morning. And then it would be too late.

A sense of hopelessness enveloped her and tears blurred her vision.

You will not *cry. You will* not *give him the satisfaction of knowing he's hurting you.*

She had to buy time.

She had to make it out alive and tell Noah she was wrong. That no store, no legacy, was worth giving up on love. If her father wanted her to keep Byrne's going, they would have to strike a compromise. She had a right to a life outside of work. She had a right to be loved and to love that someone back.

"I'll do whatever you want." Faith's mind churned through the weapons she had at her disposal. Her purse was too far to reach. Her phone was out of sight. Her briefcase abandoned by the elevator. She had one four-inch heel left. And she had her intimate knowledge of the store. She could get around blindfolded—something Griffin couldn't do since his main interest had been the balance sheets. All she had to do was get away, and she could lose Griffin in the maze that was Byrne's. "Just don't hurt me."

"Just don't hurt me," Griffin mocked and bashed his fist into her cheek, blooming bright prickles of light in her field of vision. "Why should I spare you, when you broke my heart, you slut?"

"You're my brother, Griffin."

"You don't give a crap about me." He hit her again and she crashed against a pillar, landing flat on her butt between two mannequins dressed in holiday finery. "You and your father never did."

She flailed, grasping at the mannequins' dresses to get up. "He thought of you as his son."

Griffin shoved her full force in the chest with a foot, sending her sprawling flat on the floor, breath nowhere to be found.

As she gasped like a fish, he crouched beside her and reached for something in the bag at his waist.

She crabbed away from him. Her grabbed one ankle and yanked. "Not so fast. We're just getting started."

She threw her arms out as ballast, maneuvered her weight to one side and swung her free foot at the side of his knee. She lost her remaining shoe. He fell onto the leg he held, twisting it. Something in her knee gave. With a wrench of his arm, he pinned her other leg under his weight.

As she tugged to free herself, he brought out a roll of duct tape from the pouch at his waist. "Your father married my mother because of her money, and I was the unfortunate brat that came with the cash cow."

That Byrne's had needed an infusion of cash ten years ago was true, but her father had married Rhea as much to give her a mother as to rescue Byrne's. "We welcomed you. We made you part of the family."

"Are you talking about our parents' honeymoon buying trip to Europe?" He countered her flying arms with a ram against the column that had her head spinning.

"The trip *was* a celebration of our becoming a family." Faith wedged her wrists as far apart as she could keep them while Griffin cranked the tape tighter and tighter. "We had such fun, visiting all the tourist spots—the Tower of London, the Eiffel Tower, the Leaning Tower of Pisa—while my father and your mother did all those boring business meetings. Don't you remember? We called it the Tower Tour."

"What a joke that was. We were never a family. To think I fell for it. You must have been laughing the whole time. Gullible Griffin."

When he shifted, she kicked out. He

slapped her head back into the column and the room went black for a second. He bound her ankles together with gusto. "For the past five years it's like we've been in competition. Were you jealous of me, Faith?"

"That happens between brothers and sisters." She levered herself to a full sitting position on the mannequin stand. If she could get her balance, she could find an opportunity to get away. "I was working hard to show Daddy that I was ready to take over management of the store."

"That you were better than me?" He brought his face close to hers, and she fought hard not to cringe. "And where was I going to fit in your takeover?"

"You would be CFO."

He sneered and backhanded her. "Not good enough. You were always the worst of the management snobs, treating me like a cockroach under your Manolo heels. I excused your attitude because of the way your father treated you. You didn't know better, I thought. I kept waiting for you to wake up. Do you know how many chances I gave you?"

"I didn't know, Griffin. You never told me how you felt."

"I *showed* you." He sat back on his heels. "I kept thinking you'd realize that you loved me, that together we could do something great with Byrne's. Take it to a whole new level." His mouth twisted. "But I see now I was wrong." His voice cracked. "I'm an equal, Faith. I've given as much to Byrne's as you have."

"And you're treated as an equal in my father's will." She rasped in a breath, understanding. "That's why you wanted to kill him. To get your hands on your share. Were you going to kill me, too?"

"I wanted to share it all with you."

An alarm went off in the distance, quickly followed by another.

Faith sniffed at the acrid odor filling the air. "What's that smell?"

He tipped his head and lifted half his mouth in a sick smile. "That is your destiny, Faith."

He stood her on her feet. She swayed against him. He shoved her back into the throne-like chair where a mannequin, dressed in a Byrne's private-label silver cocktail sheath, had sat on Santa's lap, whispering her silent wish list. The mannequin and Santa were now sprawled, limbs akimbo, head in the aisle, white beard and brown wig wedged in their tangled bodies. More tape yoked her torso to the chair.

"There are a dozen incendiary devices. That's a technical term, you know." He laughed at his own joke. "They'll be going off every half hour." He made a sound of satisfaction. "They'll keep the firemen so busy, they won't find you until you're nothing more than the mannequins around you. Fitting, don't you think?"

"Griffin—"

His mouth flattened to a hard line. "If I can't have Byrne's, if I can't have you, then nobody will."

NOAH RACED TO THE KNOT of firemen unrolling hoses from pumpers parked near the west-side entrance. Red lights swirled in the smoke, warping its macabre reel. Flames licked at the third floor, greedy fingers twisting in the bluster of wind feeding their hunger.

A fireman lunged at him, stopping him in his tracks. "You can't go in there."

"Faith Byrne. She's in there."

"We're on it. You gotta move back."

He reached for his phone and flipped it open. "She's not in her office." He tried to show the fireman the map of the building and Faith's position.

"We've got it under control."

"No, listen. She's not there. She's—"

"If you don't move back, I'll have you arrested." The fireman signaled an officer handling traffic control.

The officer glared at Noah. "What seems to be the problem?"

"Faith Byrne is inside. She's in trouble."

"The firemen'll get her out."

"She's not in her office." This wasn't getting him anywhere. He shoved the map in the officer's face. "She's on the first floor."

"The building's on fire. I can't let you in there."

Noah spotted a familiar face in the haze of smoke. He yanked free from the officer and dashed toward Detective Rodarte. "She's on the first floor. They're looking for her on the fifth floor."

"I got it." Rodarte ambled away toward the chief, busy barking orders.

But Noah couldn't wait. He couldn't leave Faith in a burning building, not when the firemen were looking for her in the wrong place. He had to get to her.

Forcing her to choose between him and her father. How could he have made a demand like that of her? All he'd done was hurt her, put her in an impossible position. Her father was sick. Of course she had to stay to take care of him. You didn't hurt the people you loved. You didn't put them in awkward situations. He'd been as uncompromising as Philip Byrne, and that didn't sit well.

He could learn to like a new job. And hey, there were mountains and trails and plenty of water around here. He could find a way to keep up all of his interests. As long as Faith came home to him every night, what more could he want?

Pulse pounding, every muscle primed and ready, he watched and waited, and when a break came, he took it.

Running, flying, aiming himself like a bullet, he sped into the burning building, to Faith.

"I HAVE TO, DON'T YOU SEE?" Griffin sank to his knees by the chair. "I have to make you ugly. I have to make it so nobody else ever wants you."

Griffin's rage was out of control and Faith had become the focal point of that rage. Pointing out his lack of logic wasn't going to win her any points either. Looks would be the last of her concern once she was dead.

The worst part, she realized, was that she and Griffin were suffering from the same useless exercise in futility, that they might as well be flesh-and-blood siblings. Trying to win her father's favor, Griffin had learned his controlling ways too well. They'd both spent too much time vying to gain her father's love. Having spent all of their energy trying to impress him, they'd had none leftover to discover their own paths.

And the truth was, the last ten years of her life were filled with memories of Griffin, most of them pleasant. She should have let him know she treasured having him as a brother.

When Griffin finished taping her torso to the chair, he let his head fall to her lap, exhausted from his repeated onslaught on her. Pain pounded through her body in a chorus of bruises and shrieks of cuts. Terror shook through her, but she swallowed back the fear.

Her father had rarely told her he loved her. She'd never once heard Rhea tell Griffin she loved him. Just like her, Griffin probably believed he could never earn her father's love. She should have realized a long time ago that a broken man couldn't return love.

She and Griffin had both been starved for affection, only his hunger had taken a skewed turn. If she didn't take a stand, she had just as bleak a future as Griffin's to look forward to.

Folding forward, she forced her upper body down as far as she could and kissed Griffin's head lightly. He smelled of sour sweat and tasted of salt. "I love you, Griffin. I've loved having a big brother to look out for me. Do you know how great it was to use you as a threat when some stupid jock couldn't take no for an answer?"

Faith's fear suddenly vanished and that surprised her. "I loved having you around to explore all those odd corners of the world while Daddy and Rhea went to all those boring meetings.

"I loved having you around to teach me how to drive and help me with math and with batting practice.

"I loved those burgers and fries we shared almost every Friday night while we were in college. The way I could count on you to sneak me out early from those awful charity dinners Daddy and Rhea insisted we attend. I was so glad to have you around when Gran and Rhea died. It made the whole horrible tragedy easier to handle."

"I loved all of those things, too." As if her truth got through his anger, Griffin sobbed. "I love you, Faith. Why can't you love me? That's all I wanted, for you to love me."

"I do love you. You're my brother and nothing can change that."

Griffin sat back on his heels and dabbed at her bleeding wounds with a tissue. "Why did you choose him?"

How did one explain love? Why did loving have to be so complicated? Why did it have to hurt so much? "My heart chose him. A long time ago. You know what that's like, don't you? You can't help who you love." And Noah was the man she wanted to spend the rest of her life with.

"No, you can't."

"It's not too late, Griffin. We can still get out of here alive."

He shook his head with palpable regret. "I don't think so. I'm not going to prison."

"I'll explain. I'll make everyone understand. I'll make sure we can start over."

He raked a hand through her hair, fluffing it back into place. "If I'm going to die, then I want to pick the place and time."

"We have years left, Griffin. Decades."

"We both know that's not true."

"We can make it true."

One hand cradled her jaw. "If I can't be with you on earth, then I want to be with you in heaven."

A sick sense of doom swam in her stomach. The scent of smoke was thicker. If she listened hard enough, she could almost make out the crackle of flames, the hiss of sprinklers. How long before another one of Griffin's devices went off? How long before the smoke choked her lungs? How long before the flames fused her burnt skin to Griffin's?

A strangled cry escaped her. She didn't want her last thoughts to be of Griffin. If she was going to die, she wanted to think about Noah.

But even that didn't work, because all she could feel was regret.

One more chance, she thought. *Just give me one more chance, and I won't blow it.* She would take control of her life and her father would have to accept the changes. And if he couldn't accept Noah and his part in her life…then she was ready to walk away. No legacy should hold you hostage.

In the meantime, help wasn't going to fall from the sky. If she was to get that second chance, she'd have to give it to herself.

The fire alarm had no doubt brought out fire trucks. Help was out there, just outside the doors. All she had to do was reach it.

She could do this.

Her legs, though tied together, were unattached to the chair. Though the chair looked hefty, the materials were cheap and light. After all, the only weight they were designed to hold was that of mannequins.

The fire was moving closer. The smoke was getting thicker.

She had to manufacture an opportunity. Fast.

"My throat hurts, Griffin. Could you get me some water?"

"Shh, my love," he said, leaning his head back into her lap. "Soon it won't matter."

"Could you at least loosen the tape? My hands are going numb."

"I can't let you go." His hands wound around her waist, the blade of his knife skated up her jacket, cleaving the fine wool like butter. In his tight hold, she felt his desperation.

"I'm scared, Griffin." That was no lie.

He lifted his head from her lap, eyes filled with compassion. "I could knock you out. Then you wouldn't have to be scared."

"No!" Out cold she couldn't fight, and she wasn't giving up. She wanted the future Noah had offered her. She wanted to make love to him in the moonlight again, merge their bodies, their hopes and dreams—make a baby, a family.

In the gray murk, a shadow shifted behind Griffin. As if her sheer wish had conjured him up, Noah glided silently from rounder to rounder. He stopped a short distance from them, put a finger to his lips in a sign of silence.

But Griffin must have heard the speeding of her heartbeat or felt the unalloyed joy sing through her veins, because the compassion in his eyes turned to pure hatred. With two quick slashes of the knife, he cut the tape binding her torso to the chair. "I won't let him have you. Ever."

Griffin whirled around, yanking Faith to her feet, using her body as a shield.

Chapter Fifteen

Seeing Faith bruised and bloodied, Noah died a little. He'd tracked Faith's abandoned phone through his, then let the soft lilt of her voice lead him to her through the store's gloomy light.

He wanted to dash right up to her, but he couldn't risk setting off Griffin. Falconer was always on his case about not carrying a weapon. He sat at a desk all day. He wasn't out in the field like the rest of the team. What difference did it make?

Except that right about now, he'd give anything for a loaded SIG. He'd had enough practice to know he could hit his target from here.

"Come out!" Griffin yelled. "I know you're there."

If Noah had any chance of saving Faith, he had to get closer.

"It's over, Griffin." Noah stood slowly and crossed the aisle with confidence to the grotesque holiday display Griffin had fashioned. "The police are right outside those doors."

"It doesn't matter. It's too late."

"Let her go, Griffin."

"This is all your fault." Leashed fury crackled in Griffin's eyes, in his body language. "If you hadn't come, she'd have turned to me, and she'd have seen how perfect we are for each other."

"Then kill me, not her." Standing slightly sideways, he slowly lifted his hands to show that he didn't want trouble and to give Griffin the impression Griffin was in control. He kept his voice calm, his manner unthreatening. "It's me you're pissed off at. Not her. You love Faith."

"And we're going to be together forever."

Noah inched closer. He'd much rather see that knife aimed at him than Faith's throat. "I can see that I'm outmaneuvered. But if you're taking her, you're taking me, too."

"Back off!"

In his haste to add distance between them, Griffin brought the knife forward.

Faith, bless her, took the opportunity to launch her weight sideways and break Griffin's hold on her.

With a warrior's cry, Noah slammed both his hands over Griffin's knife-wielding hand. Because he had no choice. Because Faith's life and his life were in danger, he continued shoving the knife downward, turning the blade back on Griffin, striking him in the chest with his own weapon.

Faith scrambled to her feet, hefted a chair and rammed the seat onto Griffin's back, driving the blade home. Noah fell backward and rolled out of the way. Faith landed on top of her stepbrother.

His eyes fluttered open. "Faith."

"I'm here, Griffin."

His reply was a struggle, a gurgle of words. "I didn't kill your father. Tara…"

"We found the antidote. He's going to be okay."

Griffin nodded, then with a long exhale, slumped.

Noah hauled Faith off Griffin and into his arms. He raced for the big glass doors, plunging through them and setting off another strident wail of alarms. He continued across the street and hunkered down. From here he could see all of Byrne's east side.

With the blade from his pocketknife, Noah cut Faith free. He wrapped her in his arms and planned on never letting her go. Holding her tight with one arm, he dialed Rodarte's direct line and told him where they could find Griffin, and that Faith needed medical attention.

Faith took the phone from him and let Rodarte know that Griffin had said he'd hidden a dozen incendiary devices.

Noah took the phone back. "One more thing, find Tara Widrick. She's the one who poisoned Philip Byrne."

Watching, waiting for the boys in blue, Noah rocked Faith. "It's over. You're safe now."

THE EMERGENCY ROOM DOCTOR told Faith she would need the attention of a plastic surgeon for the cut across her temple. He didn't like the two knots on the back of her head, and wanted to keep her overnight for observation.

Noah stood at the door, an immovable wall

that wouldn't let her out of his sight. The last place she wanted to spend the night was at the hospital. "Just patch what you can."

"If the doctor says you need to stay overnight," Noah said, his scowl fierce and unyielding, "you're staying overnight."

The doctor tried a softer approach. "You're a beautiful woman. Surely you won't want a scar."

She had scars that were already too deep to ever heal. The ones on her face weren't going to matter. With her eyes, she implored Noah, hoping he'd understand. "I need to go see my father."

"The nurse will call anyone you want," the doctor said.

Faith shook her head. "He's up on the third floor. He's a patient here."

"Tell you what." The doctor discarded the gauze he'd used to clean the mess that was her face. "It's going to take me a little while to round up a plastic surgeon at this hour. Why don't you go on up to see your father, and I'll page you when we're ready for you?"

Gratitude deflated her. "Thank you."

Noah helped her down from the table. "I'll go with you."

She tried to slip on her shredded jacket and finally gave up.

They said nothing on their way up to the third floor, and their silence was like a time bomb. They needed to talk, but she needed to settle things with her father first.

In the elevator she kept her eyes closed, not really wanting to see Griffin's marks on her face reflected on the doors' shiny surface. Her fist pressed into her stomach, tamping down the nausea the chime aroused. Noah's calming hand skimmed the length of her spine.

She tightened her hold on her jacket. "I'm okay."

"Of course you are."

The door to her father's room was closed, and Faith inched it slowly open so as not to disturb him. A nurse was at her father's side, tending to him.

"Hi," Faith said, hanging on to the knob. "Is this a good time?"

The nurse's head jerked up. Blond hair. Ice-cold blue eyes. Mouth, usually pouty and sexy, twisted into a cruel angle. Those weren't nurse's scrubs. Those pants where white Armani and that white sweater was a Michael Stars.

Faith gasped. "Tara."

Before Faith's exhausted body could react, Tara jerked her into the room and slammed the door shut, locking it. The force of Tara's pull launched Faith across the room. She crashed against her father's bed and sprawled on the floor.

Noah pounded at the door. "Open up!"

Tara stood above her. "What happened to you?"

"Griffin." Faith scrambled to her elbows. She couldn't do this again. She had no fight left in her. Noah's voice on the other side of the door shouted orders. He would get through. He would help her.

"Ah," Tara said with a lift of her eyebrows, "it's about time he gave you what you deserved."

"He's dead."

Tara's eyes widened, then narrowed. "You're lying."

"Why would I lie to you?"

Tara kicked Faith in the ribs. "Because it's what you do best. You strung that poor guy along for so long he couldn't think straight."

Keep her talking. Give Noah a chance to

break the door. He wouldn't give up. "What's your version of straight?"

"A merger."

Which had come first, the chicken or the egg? Had Griffin used Tara or had Tara used Griffin? Maybe she was right. Maybe they'd made the perfect merger. Faith forced herself to her knees, used the side of her father's bed to haul herself to standing.

That's when she saw the pillow over her father's face.

"Daddy?" She yanked the pillow off, but her father's features were frozen into a silent scream. His lips were blue and his open eyes were stippled with red dots.

"It's too late for Daddy dearest."

Faith searched for a pulse and found none. She checked his airway and it seemed unobstructed. She tilted his head back and, pinching his nose, breathed into his mouth.

"Oh, stop it!" Tara wrenched Faith away from her father and shoved her into the chair against the wall. "He's dead."

Someone was pounding on the door with rhythmic precision. The door bulged in and out as if it were breathing.

Faith's hands clenched and unclenched

with the desire to kill this woman. "Let the doctor in."

"I told you. Your father's dead. Has been for at least three minutes. There's no bringing him back. I was just making sure."

Hysteria climbed up Faith's throat. She refused to give up hope. Noah would get through the door. He'd get the doctor in to save her father. "Why?"

"Because your oaf of a stepbrother couldn't do anything right."

"What do you want from us?"

The glee in Tara's voice, the cant of her smile, held a sinister bent. "Why, my dear, I want everything."

"You mean money."

"That is everything."

How wrong Tara was! "Money won't do you any good in hell. You realize the only way out of here is through that door. There's no way you're getting out of this hospital without handcuffs."

Tara paced like a caged lioness. The jamb cracked, but held. The pounding resumed. She stopped, stared at the door, then whipped around to Faith. "Stand up. Nice and easy now."

"And what?" Faith snorted. "You think you can use me as a shield to walk right out of the hospital?"

"I told you to stand up."

Faith stood to her full height, facing Tara straight on. Reality was closing in on her father's killer and she was unraveling. "Griffin tried that same maneuver."

"Shut up!"

"And now he's dead."

"I said, shut up!" Baring her teeth, Tara wrapped her hands around Faith's neck, jammed her against the wall and squeezed.

Cold rage whipped through Faith. *You are not going to kill anymore. Not tonight.*

NOAH BATTERED THE DOOR with his makeshift ram. The blasted door finally caved. He crashed through the doorway in time to see Faith strike Tara's nose with a fist.

Tara shrieked and grabbed her bleeding nose.

Faith didn't stop. With a growl of pure fury, she cupped the back of Tara's head with both hands and slammed Tara's head into the wall.

Out cold, Tara dropped to her knees and

keeled forward, arms spread-eagled against the linoleum.

Doctors and security streamed in after Noah, branching off to take care of Philip Byrne and Tara Widrick.

Noah gathered Faith into his arms. "That was some right hook."

"She deserved it." Faith looked up at him, her beautiful blue eyes swimming with tears. "My father's dead."

Her head slowly swiveled toward her father, hidden behind the cadre of doctors and nurses, trying to revive him. Her hands fisted in his sweater. "Daddy's dead."

Holding her tightly, Noah pressed her head against his chest and absorbed her wracking sobs. Over her head, he silently queried the doctor who shook his head. "I'm sorry, Faith."

Noah kissed her hair, her forehead, her eyes. He'd wanted her to come to terms with her father, but not like this. "I'm so sorry."

She was exhausted, mentally, physically, emotionally, and he wished he could take all the blows for her. Tomorrow she would be in a world of hurt on all planes.

But at least she was alive. And he would be there to help her through her turmoil.

Epilogue

A month later

Faith lifted her face to the shower's warm spray, reveled in the simple pleasure of a leisurely shower after a good night's sleep.

The police had not let Noah take her home the day Byrne's had burned down. After the doctor had finished tending to her cuts, an officer had taken them to the station where they'd stayed deep into the night answering questions and giving statements.

Tara, caught with no way out, had spilled her guts, pointing the finger at Griffin. But the evidence had laid out the facts in black and white.

Griffin had sent the e-mails and gifts, but Tara, jealous of Griffin's attention to Faith, even though they were engaged and her promised boon was on the horizon, was the one who had committed all the violent acts—the slashed tires, the superglued car door, the sex chat-room setup, the bomb wrapped in a present—and set Griffin up to take the blame, just in case not everything went according to her plan.

Still, in her own warped way, she'd loved Griffin. She'd wanted to kill Philip Byrne in order to give Griffin the store. That was step one of her plan. Step two was to make sure Faith suffered an unfortunate accident—the same way Gran and Rhea had.

Griffin's first kills. He'd been angry with his mother and rammed her car over a cliff using a stolen car. Poor Gran had simply been in the wrong place at the wrong time when she'd decided to accompany Rhea to the women's club tea.

But Tara had admired Griffin's take-charge quality, and she'd manipulated that sick tendency to get rid of problems with her own carefully woven plan to take over control of Byrne's.

The piddly allowance Tara's father allotted her was crimping her social-climbing ambitions. Griffin and Byrne's were her ticket to feeding her addiction to power, influence and wealth.

Truly a relationship made in hell. They'd deserved each other.

But what Tara hadn't realized was that Griffin couldn't have handled Byrne's management alone. His vision was too narrow. He would have driven the store into the ground in less than a year. Bottom line was important yes, but building loyalty went further when it came to longevity. Even her father understood that.

The thought of her father stuttered her heart and brought a fresh round of tears. They'd never had a chance to say goodbye. She hadn't had the chance to tell him that the rules of engagement as far as the store and her future were concerned were about to change, that Noah was going to play a big part in her life. Part of her still wanted him to be proud of her decision, of the strength it would have required for her to defy him.

She hadn't had the chance to tell him that she loved him. She'd been as neglectful in that department as he had.

Even Noah's assertion that her father had told him he was proud of her wasn't enough to soothe the loss. She would always regret not having the opportunity to face him and see how those new lines would have affected their relationship.

And yet a new chapter faced her now, and she could write it any way she wanted.

Only a charred hole remained of Byrne's. She could rebuild. Or she could sell. She hadn't decided yet, and making that decision didn't seem as important as figuring out what she wanted from her life.

Faith shut off the water and stepped out of the shower. She reached for a towel, wiped the mist off the mirror and examined her face.

The bruises Griffin had inflicted had faded. Only one cut had required a plastic surgeon's nimble fingers and the scar would eventually disappear in the natural folds of her skin. The mental damage would take more time, but she was learning new facets of her strength every day.

Noah had stayed with her through her father's and Griffin's funerals, through dealing with the aftermath of the store's destruction and the crush of morbid media curiosity. She couldn't have survived so sanely without his unwavering support.

Her grandmother and her father had raised her to expect much of herself, yet in their eyes she'd always fallen short. That's what happened, she realized, when you let someone else choose your destiny.

Before now, following her own path had never been an option. And now... A whole world of possibilities lay before her.

Life was too short to spend worrying about doing everything right. She couldn't dwell on all the mistakes she'd made. She had to look ahead. She had to move forward.

She might screw up. But the results would be all hers.

And she gave thanks for her second chance.

With her father and Griffin dead and Tara behind bars, there was nothing holding her in Seattle. She could start a new business anywhere—and succeed on her own terms.

Although Byrne's was her birthright, Noah was her heart.

She slipped on a robe and stepped out of the bathroom, toweling her hair. Her steps down the hall rang with a confidence they never had before.

Noah was on the phone in the kitchen, the homey remnants of their pancake breakfast still on the counter. Who would have thought that such a simple mess would make her feel so warm and safe?

He looked up at her, his beautiful smile beaming warmth straight into every cell. A jolt of happiness hit her heart and she suddenly knew that everything would be all right. She blew him a kiss, watched yearning bloom into his eyes and reach for her across the room, filling all the broken places inside her. She could not deny she enjoyed the thrill of his response now as much as she had twelve years ago, that she wanted to feel that thrill for decades to come.

As long as she had Noah, she had everything.

NOAH WAS ON THE PHONE with Falconer, trying to make his boss understand that he would not return to New Hampshire, at least not permanently. Falconer was not taking the news well.

Faith came out of the bathroom, drying her hair with a towel. God, she was beautiful, all pink and warm from her shower, the sun streaming through the tall windows gilding her like some sort of goddess. She caught him staring at her and blew him a kiss.

His response was hot and instantaneous, and he wondered if it would ever fade. He hoped not.

"I've been thinking about a West Coast branch of Seekers." Noah had had a chance to think long and hard over the past month. Although he'd always preferred to leave the fieldwork to the other Seekers, he'd discovered, while helping Faith through the last four weeks, that he could deal quite well with the red tape that went along with interagency cooperation. He wouldn't have to give up the work he loved—he'd simply add another new dimension. The thought of recruiting members for a new team excited him. He already had a few good people in mind. "It would widen our network and allow us to help more people."

"You're our electronics expert."

A vital part of Seekers, Noah thought, but not indispensable. "My administrative skills are exactly what makes me the perfect person to start this new office."

"Who am I going to get to fill your place?"

"Hire Brynna Reed."

Falconer grumbled. "Brynna Reed hasn't left her house in thirteen years."

Not exactly true. She'd spent a week recovering from an attack at his parents' house under the able care of their housekeeper, Marta. "She was maid of honor at Reed and Abbie's wedding." With the right bait, she could be coaxed out of her safety zone. "Tell her I said the job will give her reach."

"What the hell does that mean?"

"Brynna will know. She's almost as good as me getting around electronic equipment. What she doesn't know, I can teach her. Give her a month, and you'll wonder why you thought I was so great."

"We're in the middle of a big case here, and I've already got two agents down for the count. Skyralov's stuck home with a sick kid. Chicken pox, for crying out loud. And Mercer's hand is still on the mend. I can't afford to lose you now."

"You're not losing me. You're gaining a new team." But Noah's attention was wavering. Faith had not retreated to her bedroom, but lingered at the chair in front of her desk, combing her wet hair, torturing him with memories of what they'd done in that chair and with the sight of her bare legs, peeking out of the silk of her robe. "I'll help with the transition."

"What about your family?" Noah could imagine Falconer glowering as he paced his office, his eyebrows meeting in a V in the middle of his forehead. He was reaching deep to pull emotional strings, but he couldn't know that the biggest temptation of all was right in front of him.

"I'll be flying back east," Noah assured him. As it was he didn't see his sisters more than three or four times a year, and his parents were always on some trip or other, exploring the world. "I'll probably see them more often than I do now."

Tired of running a comb through her hair, Faith stood. Her gaze locked with his and her thumbs pulled at the loose knot at her waist.

His mouth went dry.

Faith's robe slinked off her shoulders, and he gulped.

"Kingsley?"

His mind was no longer on the conversation, but on the woman approaching him, wearing nothing but a wicked smile in her eyes and on her lips.

"Kingsley?"

Noah distractedly dropped the receiver back in its cradle.

She wrapped her arms around his neck and nuzzled it. "Are you done?"

He grinned and scooped her up into his arms. "Not by a long shot."

Her fingers touched his cheek. Her eyes were intent, serious. "I could move east with you. There's nothing here holding me back."

"Byrne's is your legacy. You need to rebuild. I'm looking forward to a new challenge."

She laughed. "Me or Seekers?"

"Both."

"No regrets?"

He kissed her long and hard, not coming up for air until he reached the bedroom. "None."

"Good, because I've been thinking about wedding dates. How does April sound? The gardens will be a riot of flowers. I've always wanted a garden wedding." She teased his earlobe with her teeth.

A growl rumbled deep in his throat. "Too far away."

One hand dipped down the collar of his T-shirt and her nails raked his shoulder. "March, then? Although travel risks being tricky at that time of the year and your family—"

She gave a yelp as they fell onto her bed. He rolled until he covered her body with his and could taste the sweet spot at the base of her neck that made her eyes go all soft and wide. "Still too far."

"A wedding takes months to plan!" But her protest had no punch and her arms wound around his chest.

He cradled her face in his hands and looked deep into her eyes. "Got any plans for tomorrow?"

She laughed and the sound of it filled the room with joy as she pulled him down closer. "Apparently I'm getting married."

* * * * *

NOAH'S ORZO-RICE PILAF

4 tablespoons butter or olive oil
1 cup orzo (rice-shaped pasta)
1 cup regular long-grain rice
4 cups broth of choice (beef, chicken, vegetable, depending on main course)

In a 3-quart saucepan over medium-high heat, melt butter. Add orzo. Cook until golden, stirring often, about 10 minutes.

Add rice and broth. Turn heat to high and bring to a boil. Reduce heat to low, cover and simmer for 20 minutes or until liquid is absorbed and orzo and rice are tender.

Makes about 8 side servings.

SPECIAL EDITION

Life, Love and Family

These contemporary romances will strike a chord with you as heroines juggle life and relationships on their way to true love.

New York Times *bestselling author Linda Lael Miller brings you a BRAND-NEW contemporary story featuring her fan-favorite McKettrick family.*

Meg McKettrick is surprised to be reunited with her high school flame, Brad O'Ballivan. After enjoying a career as a country-and-western singer, Brad aches for a home and family…and seeing Meg again makes him realize he still loves her. But their pride manages to interfere with love…until an unexpected matchmaker gets involved.

Turn the page for a sneak preview of THE McKETTRICK WAY by Linda Lael Miller On sale November 20 wherever books are sold.

Brad shoved the truck into gear and drove to the bottom of the hill, where the road forked. Turn left, and he'd be home in five minutes. Turn right, and he was headed for Indian Rock.

He had no damn business going to Indian Rock.

He had nothing to say to Meg McKettrick, and if he never set eyes on the woman again, it would be two weeks too soon.

He turned right.

He couldn't have said why.

He just drove straight to the Dixie Dog Drive-In.

Back in the day, he and Meg used to meet at the Dixie Dog, by tacit agreement, when either of them had been away. It had been some kind of universe thing, purely intuitive.

Passing familiar landmarks, Brad told himself he ought to turn around. The old days were gone. Things had ended badly between him and Meg anyhow, and she wasn't going to be at the Dixie Dog.

He kept driving.

He rounded a bend, and there was the Dixie Dog. Its big neon sign, a giant hot dog, was all lit up and going through its corny sequence—first it was covered in red squiggles of light, meant to suggest ketchup, and then yellow, for mustard.

Brad pulled into one of the slots next to a speaker, rolled down the truck window and ordered.

A girl roller-skated out with the order about five minutes later.

When she wheeled up to the driver's window, smiling, her eyes went wide with recognition, and she dropped the tray with a clatter.

Silently Brad swore. Damn if he hadn't forgotten he was a famous country singer.

The girl, a skinny thing wearing too much eye makeup, immediately started to cry. "I'm sorry!" she sobbed, squatting to gather up the mess.

"It's okay," Brad answered quietly, leaning to look down at her, catching a glimpse of her plastic name tag. "It's okay, Mandy. No harm done."

"I'll get you another dog and a shake right away, Mr. O'Ballivan!"

"Mandy?"

She stared up at him pitifully, sniffling. Thanks to the copious tears, most of the goop on her eyes had slid south. "Yes?"

"When you go back inside, could you not mention seeing me?"

"But you're Brad O'Ballivan!"

"Yeah," he answered, suppressing a sigh. "I know."

She rolled a little closer. "You wouldn't happen to have a picture you could autograph for me, would you?"

"Not with me," Brad answered.

"You could sign this napkin, though," Mandy said. "It's only got a little chocolate on the corner."

Brad took the paper napkin and her order pen, and scrawled his name. Handed both items back through the window.

She turned and whizzed back toward the side entrance to the Dixie Dog.

Brad waited, marveling that he hadn't considered incidents like this one before he'd decided to come back home. In retrospect, it seemed shortsighted, to say the least, but the truth was, he'd expected to be—Brad O'Ballivan.

Presently Mandy skated back out again, and this time she managed to hold on to the tray.

"I didn't tell a soul!" she whispered. "But Heather and Darlene *both* asked me why my mascara was all smeared." Efficiently she hooked the tray onto the bottom edge of the window.

Brad extended payment, but Mandy shook her head.

"The boss said it's on the house, since I dumped your first order on the ground."

He smiled. "Okay, then. Thanks."

Mandy retreated, and Brad was just reaching for the food when a bright red Blazer whipped into the space beside his. The driver's door sprang open, crashing into the metal speaker, and somebody got out in a hurry.

Something quickened inside Brad.

And in the next moment Meg McKettrick

was standing practically on his running board, her blue eyes blazing.

Brad grinned. "I guess you're not over me after all," he said.

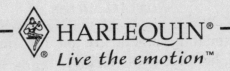

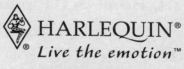

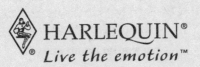

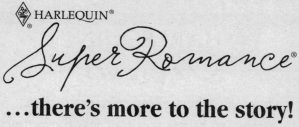

HARLEQUIN®
Super Romance®

...there's more to the story!

Superromance.
A *big* satisfying read about unforgettable characters. Each month we offer *six* very different stories that range from family drama to adventure and mystery, from highly emotional stories to romantic comedies—and much more! Stories about people you'll believe in and care about. Stories too compelling to put down....

Our authors are among today's *best* romance writers. You'll find familiar names and talented newcomers. Many of them are award winners— and you'll see why!

If you want the biggest and best in romance fiction, you'll get it from Superromance!

Exciting, Emotional, Unexpected...

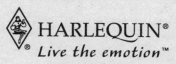

HARLEQUIN®
Live the emotion™

HARLEQUIN®
Presents®

The world's bestselling romance series...
The series that brings you your favorite authors,
month after month:

Helen Bianchin...Emma Darcy
Lynne Graham...Penny Jordan
Miranda Lee...Sandra Marton
Anne Mather...Carole Mortimer
Susan Napier...Michelle Reid

and many more uniquely talented authors!

Wealthy, powerful, gorgeous men...
Women who have feelings just like your own...
The stories you love, set in exotic, glamorous locations...

HARLEQUIN®
Presents®

Seduction and Passion Guaranteed!

Harlequin® Historical
Historical Romantic Adventure!

*Imagine a time of chivalrous
knights and unconventional ladies,
roguish rakes and impetuous
heiresses, rugged cowboys
and spirited frontierswomen——
these rich and vivid tales will
capture your imagination!*

*Harlequin Historical . . .
they're too good to miss!*

HHDIR06

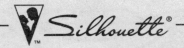

SPECIAL EDITION™

Emotional, compelling stories that capture the intensity of living, loving and creating a family in today's world.

Desire

Modern, passionate reads that are powerful and provocative.

nocturne

Dramatic and sensual tales of paranormal romance.

Romantic SUSPENSE

Romances that are sparked by danger and fueled by passion.